# A PERSPECTIVE OF DEATH

# EPISODE 3
## OF
# THE MISSING SHIELD

# Copyright:

*This book is licensed for your personal enjoyment only. This book - or any portion thereof - may not be reproduced, stored in any electronical systems, or be transmitted in any form or by any means, electronic, mechanical, photocopy, recording, or otherwise, without written permission from the publisher. Brief quotations may be used in literary reviews.*

*Also, this book may not be re-sold or given away to other people. If you would like to share this book with another person, please purchase an additional copy for each recipient. If you are reading this book and did not purchase it, or it was not purchased for your use only, then please return to your book retailer of choice and purchase your own copy.*

*Thank you for respecting the hard work of this author.*

*First published in Great Britain, May 2018*

*ISBN - 978-1-912648-04-7*

*Publisher L. L. Thomsen*

*Edited by Lesley Neale, ReVise Editing Services*

Visit the author's official website at

www.llthomsen.com

Or visit

www.facebook.com/themissingshield/

# Contents

# Acknowledgements:

To all the readers and writers out there: thank you for sharing ideas and feedback.

To my husband for his patience and everlasting support that helped me realise my goals and dreams. Though not a geek and fantasy lover like myself, your trust and generosity means the world and this work would simply not have been possible without you.

And to my children; my muses; without whom my imagination would undoubtedly still be slumbering in a deep subterranean cavern. When I spend hours at the computer you still cheer me on – never lose the magic!

# Head's up From the Author:

Hi there and thank you for hopping onboard.

I just wanted to let you know that I have deliberated and decided that I would not clutter up this book with the usual array of maps, inventories or glossaries.

Now that is not to say I don't love these things. As a matter of fact, I feel every self-respecting fantasy book should have something to support the narrative – because it's fantasy after all!

So with that in mind, I would like to direct your attention to my official website www.llthomsen.com where you may explore titbits about the world of Dallancea at your own leisure, as well as look up names, terms, maps, information about the series and of course about yours truly, also.

The journey continues, I'm immensely honoured that you are still with me. If you have liked it so far, there's more good stuff to come.

# The Story So Far

➤ Princess Iambre's best friend, handmaiden and life-shield, Solancei, has been taken prisoner by Simaro, the man she bested in an illegal jackal fight in the backyards of Old Zanzier. Cornered by his Regulators and rendered unconscious, she awakens in an old dank dungeon, her extensive injuries untended; her mind confused by a temporary memory loss brought on by a knock to the head.

➤ In her hazy state of mind, strange visions haunt her though - in particular, the recent problems between herself, Iambre and Captain Bilandro Metavo, as they and the Heiress' retinue travel towards Zanzier on the year-long celebration tour. Iambre is plagued by her affections for Metavo. The Imkarahian man bravely tries to accommodate her demands in a strictly professional capacity, however this only causes the Princess grief, which is reflected in the royal lady's increasingly inconsiderate attitude towards her staff, as well as Solancei and Bilan. Through a particularly bizarre flashback of the ensuing fight between herself and the Regulators, Solancei eventually understands what has befallen her, and manages to finally link with the State of Veranto to recover a semblance of strength just in the nick of time, before her jailor pays her a visit.

➤ Back in Iambre's royal suite, Bilan prepares to escort the Princess to an evening banquet in her honour. It's the first time he sees her after she banished him from sight and he is both elated and wary of what might happen. Deeply in love with her, he knows reality cannot allow them to know each other as lovers would, but Iambre's drive to undo his stout stance is working and he is fearful of the consequences. Iambre meanwhile is determined to beg forgiveness for her recent crude behaviour. In her heart-to-heart with Bilan, she reveals her love to him and in an ensuing argument where he hopes to push her away, passions boil over as they momentarily forget time and place in a desperate embrace that might have undone their honour, but for Bilan recalling himself.

➤ Uneasy about Zanzier after Chief Eso's report and ever anxious for her missing Shield, Iambre is filled by the sadness that she must give up the man she loves, however, she finally agrees to decommission Bilan as requested, also promising him that the necessary documentation will be his by the end of their Zanzier stay. On the back of words shared with the Chief, she seeks his advice about Zanzier and its droll Lord Zulavi, but though Bilan dislikes the place and the man, he gives her only hope. He leaves her at the banquet, their mutual affection for each other stronger than ever, but also hollow - their would-be relationship seemingly broken by the weight of truths and the demands of the unfordable gap of duties and breeding.

➢ Meanwhile, Malandar Cor'Esardan Denarlin has a revealing encounter with some Gods' honouring Humans. It reveals the truth that the Guardians' return to the Realms is a secret that cannot be kept for long, but for now he is determined to apply a stealthy guise to stay hidden from the eyes of the Mad Ones. Forced to endure a gruelling encounter with a shady horse dealer to help speed up his quest for the Twins after being forced to abandon his Eikyr, Malandar's journey continues. However, not even the fact that he finally picks up a true link by which to locate the Tarvia, can erase the growing need in him to seek out the Neidar Ba'raie as a means to arm himself magically against the coming tide.

➢ At the same time in the Elvern Realm, Sabén-Heshep, the young gifted Nefer'Kemnebit, daughter of the ruler and Descended God, Sheshem'Kufunar, bears the promise of becoming the most powerful Far Seer her people have known in millennia. It is widely believed that her Affinity will grow to rival that of the priced Tapestry – the artefact that Weaves the true history of Dallancea – but lately however, her talent has apparently gone rogue. Haunted by visions of death, dismissed by the Council for Historic Preservation as nothing more than attention-seeking fits, Nefer knows she needs help. Leaving her workroom, she strides out to locate her mother but is waylaid by the sight of her father, the Sabén-Heshep immortal Watchéran. As tradition dictates she must honour Him before she can go about her business, so acting the adult with the hope that others will look more favourable on the scope of her visions, she goes to greet Him.

# The Name of My Master?

In spite Solancei del'Isthalani Calverhana's bold pretence at readiness to face the consequences of her ill-ended jackal fight, the sudden presence of the man who'd imprisoned her made her heart plummet.

Even braced by her art, a first reflex was to avert her eyes from the tall man before her but she cut the action dead before she might reveal herself.

*It left her a little sick within.* Weirdly she realised then that she'd hoped never to set eyes on the bastard again; that she'd perhaps hoped he'd stay away; for sure, she certainly hadn't expected this sense of appraisal he appeared to emanate. It was disconcerting; out of nowhere it sent an uncomfortable pang through her, rocking the State of Veranto, and she scrambled as though she was on a climb and had just lost her footing, bracing every muscle to relax and obey so that she might rectify the mistake rather than go plummeting.

She swallowed. For a blink coldness raced through her core. *Bewitching.* Then it was gone, the Veranto smothering it. *How did he make her feel so unsettled?*

Feeling a coward, she shamefully wished that Simaro would just leave now that he'd looked at her, but instead her jailer proceeded to enter the cell with a sudden fluid purpose that found him drawing too close, too quickly. Small mercy, but at least he seemed oblivious to her burrowing twisting urge that bid her retreat from his presence. *It'd be the right thing to do, of course, but he'd laughed enough at her expense and she still had a smidgen of pride. Just a smidgen…*

Rather than give in, she fought the instinct and hardened her focus to keep her stare on the face hidden in the shadows of the wide cowl. It was an effort to ignore the fact that she reeked, and was dirty, and wet, yet she had once stared down the King himself in nothing but a dirty cutty sark after being 'lost' for a whole two days, and she'd be damned before she let this Simaro throw her where Kaimar the 3rd had not. *Damned!*

"Well, well then…" her jailer allowed after a moment of silence, the trace of jovial tolerance underlying the buff bass tone, just not one she'd dare trust though it didn't alter as he sniffed and continued, "So you're finally awake and on your feet, grey-eyes. I suppose at least you have that speaking for you, though one must say the smell is less to be desired."

As suspected he was mocking her and her heart skipped an uncomfortable beat but she managed to look straight through him.

*Well, at least I did not shit myself, what's your excuse?* Solancei wanted to insult him - though the new aberrant smell she detected in the cell did in fact not come from him. She was not in a good way though, so the words stayed with her as she drew herself up before him despite the slouch that suited her injuries better. Questions pressed: *why had he taken her here? Was she under arrest? Did he know anything about her associations? Against all possible odds, did he recognise her?*

Trust in her own voice failed her. Words could reveal too much and as Simaro raised his hands to lower the cowl, the expression on his face would've assured anyone that she should perhaps be thankful that he had dumped her here, rather than face down in River Mesatitan.

"So here's the thing grey-eyes,-" he began, shifting slightly to reveal the soft shimmer of fabric beneath his dark, wholesome cloak, "-I simply do not know whether to hang you and be done with the trouble, or whether to heed gut instincts and keep you alive for questioning."

*Hang her?* Solancei forgot to breathe. *Hang her?!*

She chewed down on her frayed lip, suddenly deeply troubled. Through a sudden disturbance within the Veranto, her whole being started quivering. *Hang…?*

He smiled coolly, pale thick brows wandering high in a parody of consternation. "By your rewarding reaction, I see that you still have some wits left to you. It softens me somewhat. Perchance, you might advise what to do with you then?"

Solancei swallowed; uncomfortably light-headed.

"You… you can't just hang people,"- she began.

"No really, grey-eyes, I can. And I will," he assured her, shifting slightly again to allow her yet another glimpse of the finery beneath his cloak. "In fact, the only thing that would prevent me from doing so - the only reason that I left you… *whole*… is because you were a hard one to measure. And so I am not yet decided."

There was no point in playing games. She regarded him with weary eyes. *What did one say to this? Did he wish for her to beg? Did he wish for her to fall on her knee before him? What?*

3

With a long unreadable look for her silence, Simaro sighed and flung back his cloak as though in readiness to draw the bejewelled slender sword dangling by his side, but instead he clasped both hands around the wide pale belt and stepped to her right, again measuring.

She endured the scrutiny; he circled behind her. She stayed still, but her shoulders seemed to ache under new strain; she could feel the weight of his appraisal. It inched over her like tiny ants, building an urge to brush herself down, and she sought for something to distract.

Rich cloth caught her eye. He had dressed well – *the realisation confounded* – in the muted colours of Zanzier sure, but the fabric of his knee-length tunic-style coat looked cut in the design of classic Etruia damask hemmed with subtle blue satin: the short raised collar and barely visible weave of chevrons within the cloth as much a part of the style as the tailoring itself. The dark breeches beneath looked soft, but not baggy, as did the pale, shin-high boots. *And as for the belt…*

Solancei looked down. For some reason his courtly appearances took her aback much like a slap in the face might have done. Somehow, she realised… somehow she'd still expected him to be wearing the plain, functional clothes of a jackal fighter rather than those of a courtier, and for a heartbeat her hold on the State of Veranto quivered as her disadvantage hit deeper still. He looked neat: dressed for a banquet. She was covered in drying filth, smelling of sweat and leather and something better left unsaid. *What she*

4

*wouldn't have given to face him after a bath and with a clean set of clothes too!*

"So what will it be, grey-eyes?" he enquired lightly, appearing on her left, looking pristine and elegant, "An extended visit? Or the noose?"

Scrambling her meagre resources to hold on to the Veranto link, she wasn't sure what to say, nor how long she could continue to do this, but...

Raising her eyes to his, she tried not to shudder. *Out in the backyards it had been easier to forget that he was not just a common thug with no real power, but here...*

His white-blond hair had once more been styled, he wore gold on two fingers, and though his carved features remained somewhat muted, they still portrayed the sobering quality of a Lord just the same – an impression that was backed of course, by his fine outfit and expensive cloak. *He's a flecking, cheating rat all the same too, of course - and yet you're still the one who's been locked up, not he. Klaas will never straighten this mess in time! He'll hang you without a second thought if given reason!*

Solancei drew a halting breath, understanding something must have betrayed her thoughts when she saw his lips quiver with the sentiment of imminent victory.

She hated giving in, but-

*Oh what the fleck...*

"What would you have of me?" She relented, barely able to withhold resentment, yet pleased that her voice had not been reduced to a croaking squeak.

His smile widened. It looked the most genuine she'd seen so far, but she hated the revelation of triumph in his eyes.

"For starters: the name of your tutor in the Arts," he informed, pausing to face her.

Forestalling her words as she shook her head with feinted confusion, he said, "Nah grey-eyes, do not play with me now. I offered you a choice out of interest, not mercy. Pretend ignorance again and we will no longer be keeping this civil. Understood?"

*Civil?* Solancei resisted the urge to snort with sarcasm as his 'misconception'. *But it was true: he could do as he pleased. She had to get smart; think like a Shield!*

"Very well." She sighed, closing her eyes for a brief moment as though the words cost her. *In a way they did, but not as he thought.* Her mind was racing. He didn't want games, but it seemed to her that this was already one giant gamble. *How the irony laughs at the irony...*

Very well," she repeated, a note of resignation creeping into her voice, "but pray tell me first: just how long has it been since the fight? How long have you kept me here?"

For a moment she thought she'd pushed her luck yet again, but then he offered her a nod of agreement. "You choose well, grey-eyes, and as a courtesy I will allow you a boon. You ask how long you have been here? Well, you have been in the lands of dreams and beyond for longer than I expected. Today is Geistmarsday. It's late. Right before the hour of the lazy merchant, I believe."

For a moment, the casual words seemed to rock her world as they sank in. Then she blinked.

"Geistmarsday?" She echoed. Shocked. *A whole day. A whole day and half of another... gone! No wonder she'd pissed herself! She'd missed the first banquet; spectacularly so - not to mention most of today! Fleck but Iambre would be frantic!*

"You look alarmed," he quipped with incidental lightness, "I apologise for the lateness of my call but don't tell me now that you had somewhere more important to be?"

His denigrating smile made her want to smack him, but linked with the Veranto the need was breezy.

"Nowhere important," she lied, staring at him with feinted calm, "only the need to be anywhere else but here, I guess."

She swallowed and looked away but suddenly not even the State of Veranto could calm the storm of anger brewing in the pit of her stomach. Barely able to control herself, she raised her stare to his, this time not afraid to let the incredulity flow.

"Gods man, I won the flecking jackal fight!" she protested. "Why the need for this? That Regulator of yours needn't have kicked me when I was already down! Your whistle guy needn't almost have taken my head off my shoulders. You realise those crazy antics might have killed me!"

At her words, Simaro shifted slightly as if to shake himself off her ire and her eyes were drawn by a flicker of colour as small jets of light sprang off the faceted stones decorating the scabbard and sweeping hilt of the ornate-looking sword by his left hip. *The dark glory of garnets or rubies,* she thought, for some reason seeing Iambre in her mind's eye: beautiful and ready for this evening's banquet. It struck her with a pang and she very nearly leapt for the weapon then, but the mad idea that she could somehow fight her way free, died before it was even half-formed. *He'd seen the direction of her gaze. He must know as well as her, how tempting an offer he'd extended!*

Angered at her own lack of discipline, she wiped her face clear of emotion and looked up.

"Are you quite done?" Simaro cocked his head, his mouth dragging wide to deepen the short smile lines and convey an almost sympathetic expression for her persistently poor timing. When she favoured him no answer, he simply shrugged as if he had expected no less.

"It's surprisingly easy to get the wrong ideas when you are desperate," he commiserated, "And maybe... just maybe, you *could* do it. I confess - even if we keep this just between you and I now – that you really were quite good dancing that Jackal. So efficient one might say, that it sparked my lingering intrigue.

"See your lack of respect was puzzling: where others might have grovelled, you continued to insult, and - quite unlike the Zanzierian women who know their place - you did not seem to care. I tell you grey-eyes..."

Halting mid-sentence he buried her under a wily look, as though a predator about to determine whether to trust in the scent of a new path, or whether to stick to the already well-known deer-trail. He did not seem to have reached a definitive conclusion, when he finally said, "Well, perplexing though it may be, I still don't know if all of this deviance makes you ignorant, or brazen, or...? Or something else, indeed. Yet, in any event, understand that my curiosity is what has kept you breathing thus far. I would advise you not to ruin it!"

Solancei inclined her head a fraction. She understood the warning, yet chose to see it as a compliment.

"Ignorant or brazen, I have been called worse, and if either offends,-" she lifted her bound hands as if to remind him of his own actions, "-I am hard-pushed to feel regret. I am but a product of my environment. If I am offensive, then take it to my Master. You ask to know his name? Well, let me warn you that my Tutor in the Arts rules the world and He would frown upon my weakness if I were not as I am!"

Sensing the truth in her words, yet clearly not understanding, Simaro sniffed in question. "And just what is that supposed to mean? You are in Zanzier girl! Observe our traditions and know your place! You should have paid attention to the small differences we admire in this province, before embarking upon this path!"

"Oh I know very well what you 'like' in this Gods-forsaken part of the world,-" Solancei retorted dryly, "-but I do not offer respect where none is given!"

"Is that a fact?" Simaro laughed darkly, revealing an edge of sordid delight. "Well I guess we'll just have to change your philosophy then."

"You will change nothing,-" she promised with a darkness to match, "-least of all me. It's a free world!" *And what would King Kaimar think of your archaic views?* She nearly added. *Does he even know?*

"When you break the law by entering an illegal sport, the world becomes less free, grey-eyes," he countered and Solancei felt a sliver of anger curl in around her hold on the Veranto.

"Verily? And yet I see no string around your wrists!" She stabbed, cocking a meaningful eyebrow. "I am just a single woman. Am I really that much of a threat to your way of living?"

Simaro barked a laugh, flashing teeth. "Gods no grey-eyes, you flatter yourself. But you are a curiosity bearing promise! A promise of something I've been looking for, shall we say. Now give me the name of your Master! Tell me who helped you culture this very adequate mastery of the Art of Kizano? Tell me who taught you to progress past the lower grades of Veranto! As my eyes do not deceive, you are holding a Link right now – and very skilfully too. It is all-in-all, an impressive bag of talents for one so young, which means that you will be nothing short of special to them."

*Them…*

Solancei looked into his pale speculative eyes and wondered if he'd ever let her leave or simply not just take what he wished and cut her down. She had no guarantees. Her anger seemed a small, impotent thing. She could not tell him what he wanted to know of course – it was beyond question - but how much did he already know?

A stab of desperation made her struggle to control herself from attacking him then and there in a way that would have them both rolling ungracefully on the floor within just a blink, but she managed to cling to calm because she saw her own defeat in such rash action.  In their current position, he would simply use his superior bodily strength to flip her over and then she'd have achieved nothing. Kizano would not give her enough leverage to win free; he was waiting for her to do something, and she just wouldn't play into his hand. *But she could lie; extend the gamble she'd already begun: she'd just dropped a hint before, and he already thought her of New Wood descent…*

"Who is your Master?! Who taught you?!" Simaro's fist shot out, clamping to the soft column of her throat like a vice. "Names! Facts! I will have these now!"

Solancei gagged, shock parting before anger as it rose like bile to course through her veins - back at the jackal fight he'd caught her similarly, and this time – *hang or not* - she did not wish to give him quite the same satisfaction.

She made herself go pliable under his grip. *It seemed to annoy him. Small pleasures…*

"You will answer my questions," Simaro repeated with a strange fervent light in his near-colourless eyes, "Now do not lie to me! Anyone who practises the moves from the fifth Karta of Kizano has a Master! Anyone who shows your flair with a haitu has a Master! Anyone who knows how to drink from the *Fountain of Veranto* has a Master – and I, will know his name!"

Simaro's fingers seemed on the verge of drilling holes in her skin but with his last words echoing in her mind, Solancei nevertheless felt an influx of such enormous relief that she almost fainted.

*He did not know her!* She was certain now. *Which in turn meant that he did not know of Klaas or of her ties to the Crown*

*Princess! It labelled Iambre safe from repercussions and Klaas likewise…*

"My Master - you ignorant churl,-" she hissed somewhere between the need for breath and the edge of madness, "-is the Destroyer of Life, the Ruler of Man and War: Anchan'Chi the Majesty of All End! Shall I continue?"

*Gratification followed.* For a flicker of a beat, Simaro went stiff as a frozen corpse, his eyes widening imperceptibly. Then he released her as though burned and she fell back from him breathing coarsely as she clasped her throat awkwardly and sought to relieve the fire within. Oddly the Veranto did not seem to soothe the abuse quite as she was familiar, but she was too distracted to truly care. *She still held the link; her other injuries were masked as before and she could not waste her advantage.*

Keeping her stare steady, she noted his lingering dilemma. *This might work…*

Massaging her throat for a moment longer, she croaked, "His Name is spoken and I am His disciple. I act according to the gospels of Anchan'Chi of War; I travel for self-awareness; with my skills I honour Him. Now, what would you do to appease Him?! Your demands have brought His attention down on us without cause! It's a development sure to offend Him as will your opinion of my status! Save grace! Remove my bonds and repent!"

The lie was smooth; the demands easy: the words flowed straight off her tongue without even the slightest quaver. To offend any deity was to call down disaster any time of day, but to touch one of their Anointed was to risk them turning their back on you.

Solancei often did not know what she'd done to offend the entire Parthenon so: they all seemed oblivious to her existence, mostly she lived well-enough without the benefit of their attention and did not care, but Simaro would differ.

"Anchan'Chi?" Simaro breathed in pale-lipped question, a spasm travelling down the sinews of his muscular neck, "But that… that's impossible."

He hovered for moments before regaining control of himself but his voice had betrayed an edge of lingering bafflement, which tied to just the correct character of concern.

Watching her with caution fluttering like a low flame of an oil lamp about to burn dry, he seemed to grow pensive, yet then his unease spluttered one final time as he killed the emotion, retaining only a glimmer of weariness as his gaze travelled the breadth of her face one final time. Unlike before, she could read his decision before he shook himself and looked briefly at his guards, then pinned her with a gaze of slight admiration. *This wasn't going to stick…*

Crossing his arms he shifted his weight and exhaled as though in troubled relief. Then a small trickle of laughter escaped him.

# To Hang or Not to Hang…

*Why the laughter?*

For a moment Solancei wondered if Simaro had lost his faculties all together but his eyes were hard and focused.

"You are something else all right," he allowed eventually with a note of amused incredulity. "Something else and something more! You see, I almost believed you there, grey-eyes. And for me to offend Anchan'Chi…? Well, it would never do, now would it?"

Scratching his chin, he rocked on his feet as though in further deliberation or indecision, then he stilled.

"Well… it's been a while since a wily trench of your calibre tried something as stupidly ignorant as a personal challenge! This… this could be interesting."

Speaking quietly as though to match his mood, his words were nevertheless skewed by a new darkness she could not decipher the origins of. It sent chills through her tenuous hold on the Link though, and to uphold her small charade though she feared it suddenly useless, she appeared to bristle at his denial. *He'd stood ready to believe her? What had changed?*

"You know of course, that I have a certain affinity with the good Lord Anchan'Chi, I suppose? That I have a shrine dedicated to Him above all others; that I revere His words and strength, but-"

Shaking a finger at her like some benign schoolmaster, he spoke quietly but forcefully, "But something makes me wonder about your allegiance, grey-eyes. You see, I note that you don't bear His mark upon your shoulder and I most assuredly recall how the priests brand you girls immediately upon speaking the words of fealty, so…"

Solancei closed her eyes. Within the link of Veranto, there was peace and nothing: an endless field of pure serenity. It offered escape; she'd probably need it; she certainly needn't gaze to the tear in her shirt that exposed her unscarred shoulder to reveal the truth. *Fleck! He'd hang her and-*

"But I have a good feeling about you, grey-eyes. A good feeling!" The lilting lift of his voice forced her attention outward. *The State of Veranto made her feel numb, but strangely not distant now.*

"You hold secrets worth knowing, I think." he continued. "Your convincing lies tell the tale that it must be so and I will take on your challenge then, grey-eyes. And I will make excellent sport of your charming presence, have no fear. Talk today or talk after I persuade you. It really is much the same to me!"

Turning on his heel, Simaro clasped the hilt of his flashy rapier and strolled towards the door just as Solancei pounced after him. A soldier's sharp sidestep halted her as much as the sudden gloved hand against her sternum.

"Sport?" she shouted at his back, bobbing slightly sideways and ignoring the hand, "What in the realm are you saying? Let me out of this flecking hole, you boar! I insist! I won the challenge! You cannot keep me here without charge and we both know you cannot charge me without implicating yourself! Pox on you! Who do you think you are?!"

Stopping in his tracks as though she'd struck him a physical blow, Simaro turned to face her. A silent communique saw the soldier retreat to his former place and she caught just the faintest hint of lost patience in the arrogant rejection he seemed to channel her way as though she was incidental to his decision.

With a voice veiled in softly-spun anger and new contempt, Simaro sneered in disdain. "Woman, who am I? *Who am I?* Listen to you. There you go again with your attitude: like only a spoiled rich lady would dare!

"Who am I? Well you should have figured by now that I am the one who can do whatever I damn well please! I *own* this town – *this province* – and every single person within it, so if it pleases me to add you to that list, then that is precisely what I will do!"

He smiled; a cruel gesture of his own certainty. "Now if you *are* indeed 'nobody', well then nobody will care. But if not, then my sport will just have doubled since someone is bound to show up eventually asking questions. However, in the meantime, why don't we see how far we can get on our own, shall we?"

A wave of aversion rushed her, crushing itself against the serenity of Veranto as she took first one, then two steps forward. The soldiers shifted but Simaro gave them a look and they stilled. *His words made no sense. Sick people did these kinds of things. Sick, scarred people!*

*She'd been determined to escape him before; now she realised she must!*

Burning with the need, she decided to call halt to the man's amusement.

16

"I will be no one's sport, of that you may rest assured," she promised, surprised by the calm determination riding upon every one of her words. Lowering her tone further, she continued with unveiled warning, "Oh and I will speak with you now, only as a reminder that Anchan'Chi is not the only god out there! They will all be watching your actions here today with ire and judgement. Your conduct is illegal; this will damn you all in their eyes!"

Solancei saw him pause then. If he had not believed her lie before, at least this saw a new flicker of uncertainty penetrate his veneer, but it lasted only a heartbeat.

"You speak with a persuasive tongue grey-eyes," he allowed, "but I hear the note of consternation in your voice. If the Gods decide to judge my actions, so be it! Yet, I rather think they might be as fed up with all the rules and laws as the rest of us! Perhaps they will not judge against me, but in favour? Perhaps they shall derive enjoyment from this entertainment and forgive me my indiscretions accordingly? In any event it matters not, for there is also the little matter of payback, so really…"

Solancei blinked. *Astounded.* "Payback? What payback? I didn't rob your treasury nor steal your favourite horse. I won a jackal fight. There is no payback! The very thought goes against everything the jackal fights ever stood for!"

"Ah well, this is Zanzier." Simaro grimaced as though to hide anger behind a smile. "And here there *is* payback, girl! Nobody shows me up in front of my people without regret – quite frankly, it undermines my authority and that is unforgivable, no matter who you are. Hope you found that small rebellion of yours worth it – the rest belongs to me!"

Sure of himself, Simaro ignored her confounded stare and turned smartly to retrieve one of the torches from its wall bracket. Solancei gritted her teeth to arrest her tongue. She wanted to jump the cocksure rat but something unrealised stopped her before she could react on her rash instinct, because deep inside, a foreign, little known part, shied away from the task. Stupidly, she realised that she was fearing her own ability; fearing that it might somehow worsen her injuries. *His men stood ready; the walls seemed to move, and they hadn't a moment ago; she feared that he would simply just win again. Could she 'survive' another knock?*

She didn't like the answer that sprang to mind, nor the idea of his condescending supremacy in the event of such a development! That would be more than she could possibly stomach – yet regardless, somehow she had to gain more time!

In frustrated outrage against her own cowardice, as well as her anger at his damnable behaviour, she spat after him instead.

"So you presume to know the will of the Gods?" she vented in frustration at the back of his head. "You dare challenge Their Authority? You will be forgiven nothing if you harm me any further, you flecking snake-son! Nothing!"

*And there it was again…*

The irony of her words was fleetingly obvious since she herself had no close relationship with any god and thus stood in poor position to lecture on presumptuous ideas in the first place, but nevertheless her words appeared to have an impact on the guards, for they shifted uncomfortably as if their names had just been called to question. Simaro, however, only laughed, "We shall see, shall we not? By your words, perhaps it is not the Gods I need fear in the event of your ruin, but rather someone much less celestial, eh?"

For a beat Solancei's heart stood still, insight cloaking her in fear that not even the State of Veranto could mask.

"Come!" He proceeded to command the men at the door. "But leave them a light."

Stooping through the exit to spearhead his odd coterie of silent, cloaked men, Simaro sidestepped and hung back to let them file past till the oppressive darkness returned in a way that one remaining light was not able to alleviate. Thinking furiously, Solancei looked down at her bound hands but she seemed to have hit a citadel wall. Nothing she could say would be enough to sway him. *He'd keep her no matter what - and suddenly she did not want Klaas and her men to start poking their noses around. If Simaro should learn, the link would be too obvious: too, too obvious - yet on the other hand...*

Solancei daren't even think what would happen if they didn't come for her. *She had to get out of here! Gods, if she were not back before it was time for Iambre's retinue to leave town, then what?* They'd arrived on Ganorsday, frightfully delayed according to schedule. That had been due to Iambre's stubborn wishes for a detour into the Wilderness – an event that hadn't been further improved by the fact that when they'd finally arrived, it had been evening, not morning - and yet another two days later than the already amended plans had specified! The additional delay had cut

19

their intended stay from twelve days to ten. *And now it was Geistmarsday. Three days gone already...*

Indecision flared but what could she do? The answer – *it would seem* – was 'nothing'.

"You two,-" Simaro's voice cut into her thoughts, surprising her, as he addressed the lingering men, "-bring the blade-whore would you? But have a care not to damage her any further – she won't speak too prettily with another crack in the head, you hear!"

Ducking away from the exit, he appeared to change his mind, delaying his own departure to bob back round, "Oh yes, and a word of warning to you both: do not let her size fool you! This one needs shackles. If she's trouble then do what you must but nothing permanent. Indeed, do try to remember that she is not like the women we are familiar with."

Offering her a brief cheerful glance, Simaro disappeared, leaving the hallway beyond the door in renewed darkness but Solancei barely noticed as she stared at the now suddenly open path before her. *The keys remained in the door – untouched. Perhaps there was a chance...*

Interrupted, as the two remaining guards swivelled towards her in strange synchronicity, Solancei looked away from the door, her mind spinning with more than balance issues. To her, the two gaolers looked as though they were trying to approach a rabid dog finally cornered, but to their credit, they both showed just enough caution to indicate intentions - and they were following their Master's orders to the letter.

She watched them with a weary sense of resignation. Despite the Veranto, she felt tired. Under her wide wrist-bracers, her forearms seemed all too heavy: as though they were already encircled in irons. *Could she make her hands work?*

Flexing her fingers, she felt detached from her own skin, but she had a flash decision to make! Either she could let Simaro do this… Or else elect to fight her way free now and take her chances. It was not a hard choice, but still…

Solancei retreated a small step, then another, to allow herself enough room to manoeuvre. Both men were big and ugly – maybe none too bright looking, but undoubtedly capable, and muscular enough beneath their cloaks, she saw. *As though they spent most their time wrestling oxen. But it mattered not. Skill – not brawn - would see her through this.*

She composed herself. She wasn't sure exactly what to do, but when one of them sent her a crude smirk and a knowing wink – she suddenly had her answer.

From the way his eyes seem to glitter, she was reminded in a flash of the way her sodden, tired laces had loosened to make her normally well-fitting blood-oxen breeches hug her hips indecently low; her still-damp, partly ripped flaxen shirt must reveal just enough flesh to complete the appeal regardless of her leather jerkin, and…

*And Gods, but this had better work!*

Apprising the two men as they carefully circled closer from either side, Solancei's eyes flickered between them and fell for a split heartbeat on the man she'd already dubbed 'Winker'. He noticed, of course, and chose that very moment to casually flash open his cloak to reveal the presence of a long-bladed basic knife strapped to the left side of his belt. With a slow grin, he let the fabric fall back into place and Solancei understood his silent threat just perfectly. *Winker was nothing but a stupid bully and she did not let her eyes linger.*

Still, the oaf was thoroughly mistaken if he thought her impressed by the small show of this 'supposed supremacy' though. If there was one thing that didn't intimidate her, it was a presence of weapons and instead her mind had already incorporated the blade into her emerging plans; a bull seax was a serviceable weapon when in close combat, unrefined but dependable; it would cut the cord on her wrists as well as any blade, and her hatching plan solidified further.

She sincerely hoped that she'd read Winker correctly, though. Sure, his behaviour seemed hard to misinterpret certainly - but this was not exactly her forte – and with an inward cringe she prayed she'd never have to share the details of this event with anyone; she could just imagine the look on Iambre's face-

Solancei blinked. She didn't have to like it, she decided, but needs must and all that, and before she could change her disposition, she drew the State of Veranto tightly 'around' her so as to exclude all else. *Only one thing for it then...*

Changing her stance in an apparent show of surrender, she stuck out her right hip just enough to remind both men that beneath the layer of grime, she was still a woman, and whatever she'd expected, she was still amazed at the near-instant affect her change of pose appeared to instil.

She smothered the urge to giggle as it pressed against the bubble of Veranto, and watched in wonder as the first hint of lurid understanding flashed cross Winker's shadow-laced features. She certainly didn't have a barmaid's charming endowments, nor the comely attire of a whore to display her attributes, and yet the man seemed suddenly very amenable nonetheless. *Men! Gods, but Ina was right: 'predictable' was not the word! Yet, best not think...*

To ease them further into the ruse, she bent her lips into a suggestive smile even though the effort almost killed her resolve.

"Now, now lads... there is no need for that kind of care," she purred, somehow managing to soften her voice. "I will come along as you gentlemen please."

Smiling at both of them in turn, she shrugged and made a point of flashing her bound wrists as she patted back a few wavy strands of escaping hair with a disarming gesture.

"Why the creeping?" she added for good measure, widening her smile. *And at least she still got a good smile.* "I don't bite, you know; in fact, as you can see, I am wholly pacified, most assuredly at your disposal, and there is nothing to say we cannot have a measure of fun before we go."

Nodding her head towards the space left empty when Simaro had departed, Solancei made sure to widen their understanding. "Surely *he* is not waiting around for you lads to heel - and I won't tell if you don't?"

The men shared a look. She was dearly hoping that she was right and that Simaro was on his way and not just waiting ten yards down the corridor but that it was a chance she'd have to take. For now, she had a task to complete, and for her design to work she needed to get Winker to forget his master's words and come closer. *Really close…*

Nodding meekly at him as if in shy encouragement, she ignored the growing, nervous chill that captivated her insides as he filed closer. His rank smell of what might be slave tobacco mixed with old sweat, fermented the air. *Veranto don't fail me now…*

Solancei drew in a breath and entered a state of she might have dubbed 'dispassionate calm'.

There was no chance that they'd miss this opportunity now that she'd let them imagine it – she saw it in their changing behaviour, in the shift of their bodies, in the rising gleam of excitement in their eyes, and she'd listened to enough of Ina's stories, seen enough men leer at Iambre, to know what they were thinking now.

A tight cage squeezed her heart.

Without the State of Veranto, she might just have vomited at the prospect of their intentions. She was not a trollop, nor a trench, or a charmstress; as a matter of fact, she'd never done anything this 'bold' before, but it would work because she wanted it to. *Simaro had called her brazen – and she was - but without the Veranto…*

As though charmed by the very thought itself, the 'muscle' on the left had all but stopped his approach in favour of looking her over as if he were suddenly seeing her for the first time. He was the one who'd stepped in to restrain her before, but while he was simply ogling now, Winker was holding true, drawing nearer. *Yes, she'd have to be brazen…*

"Don't hang back. Come over here and get started?" She encouraged in her most bewitching tone so as to suit the suggestion, simultaneously suppressing a shiver that wormed through her Veranto armour.

Winker exhaled sharply, a charged expression travelling over his squared, ruddy features and her revulsion grew an instant notch. *That man was more than prepared to accept her 'invite'. It was almost too easy.*

"So," he grated just shy of a whisper, "you are a wild one, are you? You are the one who put Oran in the poor-house? Well… I don't see how."

*Oran?* Solancei had no idea what he was on about but still she chose to shrug with a self-denigrating modesty. "Ah M'lord, nothing but an exaggerated rumour, I'm sure."

"Why, exactly!" Winker retorted. "Now I don't see what the fuss is about. Mitail told us how he folded you with that blade – left some pretty 'makeup' behind too, didn't it. Oran, the stupid pie-brained oaf, must have fallen and cut himself or something."

With half a look to his wingman, Winker honked and spat on the ground. "If not, then the man was an idiot if he let a small foreigner take him. Ain't that so, Barow?"

"Sure," came the reply from the other man, but Solancei saw that amidst their exchange, neither of the two seemed to care overly much about Oran's supposed plight. *Oh joy…*

With a dirty smile, Winker returned his attention to their prisoner, drawing back the tight cowl of his cloak with slow deliberate care. Solancei wished he hadn't. The torch highlighted an almost shaven head with a handful of bald spots where vermin had plagued the skin unsympathetically. A puckered vertical scar crossing the left side of his skull worked well to strip Winker of all remaining charm, and if his age was irrelevant, her nose rebelled at his general lack of sanitation. Stale ale, something sweet, rank oily dog, mildew and… and old sweat - the additional aromas assaulted, worsening the bouquet as he paused, broad and solid before her.

*We both stink like ripe middens, but at least I have an excuse,* she thought, pulling an agreeable face as she tried to breathe less. If she gagged it might be over, but perhaps he saw now only what she'd offered, not what she felt, and it hardly mattered anyway. It was almost time…

Sending him another, if slightly less sleek smile, Solancei could have spared herself the pretence: the man did not seem bothered whether her original invitation was still standing. Winker was paused on the cusp of reaching out, savouring something she preferred not to think about - then the gaoler leant in, his presence ramming her feet to the floor with imaginary nails that prevented retreat.

Winker ejected another of those strange sharp breaths staring at her throat, but then his eyes rolled to her face. *Malignant interest, and-*

She expelled a harsh puff of air of her own and he offered her a conspiratorial, black-tobacco edged smile of lewd promise. With a cold flicker of alarm, she noted his hand gliding minutely towards the seax.

"I prefer mine screaming," he told her without blinking, low voice twisting with hard excitement as his eyes appraised her for signs of reaction, "Will you scream for me, precious?"

Solancei couldn't make herself speak. Even with Veranto smothering her emotions, all initiative seemed to have left her but Winker led the way just the same.

Stepping uncomfortably close, the man was but a blink away from touching her and she sensed then that he was aiming to clasp her arms to ensure her co-operation.

*Pulse exploding, revulsion descended like a smothering blanket. Gods...*

"So tell me wench, will you scream for me?" he prodded, stroking the loose wisps of her long plaits back past her shoulder with the edge of his hand - and in that split moment, she had the unfortunate pleasure of adding the unpleasant smell of his rotten breath to the list of odours. His face was so close to hers now that the impression of his the days-old whiskers might be imprinted upon her cheek. *What was she doing? Mercy...*

"Oh honey, there'll be screams..." she whispered near his ear, her lips stiff but the tone so honeyed that she barely recognised it as her own, when his hands began to touch down the length of her upper arms. Faltering for a blink, she picked up resolve, reiterating, "There... there will be screams, just... just not mine!"

Like a striking falcon, Solancei clasped a fist full of cloth at the neckline of Winker's cloak, driving her left knee twice into his groin.

As she'd imagined, the dreams of fallacious pleasure deserted Winker with the hiss he expelled as he literally dwindled in size, momentarily taken by agony.

Further relief buoyed as she felt his fingers lose their strength, trailing off her arms with the transfer of a sharp spasm. *That was her window. Her five breaths of gaining the upper hand, and then-*

Without pause, Solancei let her hands abseil down the length of fabric, floundering to reach the exact spot beneath his ruffled cloak where she'd seen the knife strapped to his belt. *Almost she thought it an impossible task. Her hands were numb; the man was crumbling away from her; she couldn't see!*

Her palm connected with the handle of the knife just a tick before desperation could strike but then she sensed the hardness, the change in texture that it represented, and willed her bound hands to co-operate. *Again, it almost didn't happen.* It seemed forever until she finally held the blade; Winker was wheezing - debilitated only through the pain in his genitals and the shock of her violence, but already fumbling to deny her - and she elbowed him in the face, almost by accident and rather without finesse.

The surprise of it seemed enough to cut up his interference, however, and she shoved him off in a beat then, shifting to land one mud-painted boot solidly just below his ear in a likewise less than refined Kizano kick that saw her stumble sideways from loss of balance and the sudden appearance of trapped fireflies in her head.

Barow jumped to intercept with a thin animal growl of anger then, launching himself across Winker's crumbled form with an intensity that might have mirrored a drunken berserker. She shifted to align herself with new purpose, grunting as his swing for her face caught her shoulder.

*It was all she gave him. Out of necessity. One swing; not as a courtesy; not as some misguided notion of fairness, but as a necessary concession...*

As she'd known, he swivelled like a bear and swung again, but she was moving and his eyes went agog when she glided underneath, caught his arm with a clever twist of *'viper rising; sparrow escaping'* to land him crouching at her feet with a crack of bones and a yelp of everything right with the world.

Pain fuelling the anger, Barow twisted, grabbing for her with his still-good hand; she could not feel her own fingers but she slashed down with the seax regardless then, striking, and realising that her blow had hit true only when Barow released her with the curdling yelp of a muzzled injured dog to retreat from danger with a score across three knuckles and a deep, crooked line ascending his wrist. *Blood welled; seemed to be everywhere in a blink. Stomach heaving, her vision rippled.*

Solancei shook her head, clearing the dancing lace from her peripheral view. It hadn't been there before and as Barow retreated, she did too. She had half an eye on the exit, hoping the sound of their struggles hadn't travelled, but then she noticed Barow follow her gaze.

Alarmed, she saw his expression turn in mean calculation. *In a blink he'd give away her advantage and then...*

Ignoring the danger to her own health, she bounced, spun and kicked, and the fiend sagged forwards, nothing more than a soft syllable escaping him as he folded into his own world of dark stars and fireflies. *It still left 'Winker'.* He was moving - she'd kept him on her right – but he seemed stunned.

Solancei shifted and turned for the cell door. She still feared that the other men must have heard the commotion and would be returning to stop her, but the State of Veranto seemed to blaze like a beacon of warmth within her, fuelling her resolve and her strength, and she let the heat roll in her veins so that she didn't have to notice her body's strained protests at the vigorous activities she'd pressed herself to perform.

*So let them come! She would not allow them to take her again!* Faster than a speeding fox going to ground, she was through the door - and without further thought for what she might encounter beyond, she slammed the pathetic array of wooden planks shut on the two guards, cranking the key round twice to seal the lock.

It was a poor thing to rely upon to keep anyone locked away for long but she wasn't looking for more than a few moments. Urgency spilt through her core, but not the desperate kind that would've fuelled her without the State of Veranto. Instead, it was like an infection that egged her to push herself; to rid herself of this place because she suddenly had the means – yet as a seasoned player with such heady pitfalls of the Veranto, she forced the impulse down to pause and take stock.

It was easily done. A dark corridor ran before her in either direction. It was empty, but to the left she was still able to spy just the faintest glimmer of what she took to be the torches belonging to Simaro. *She hadn't long before it would fade from view…*

Cursing herself an idiot, she thought of the perfectly good torch she'd left on the other side of the door, but she was all too keenly aware that she did not wish to be left behind to fumble along unknown corridors in the black. *She must hurry!*

Heart racing, Solancei licked her sore lips and looked at her weapon. *Just one more thing to do…*

Shifting the seax in her grip so that the keen edge would face the floor, she stuck the handle between her knees, looped her hands over the tip and ran her bound wrists down the long blade. Upon her second workings, the rope twanged and loosened.

She looked down the corridor. By now, the light had all but disappeared and her heart was racing with the need to catch up. *If she lost the light… if…*

Snatching up the knife and sucking in a breath, she shrugged her hands free of the severed lengths of twine, so very pleased that the pain released with the renewed flow of blood seemed little more than an added twinge within the State of Veranto.

Then she ran.

# By the Watchéran's Table

For a heartbeat, the Sabén-Heshep Best-Loved Daughter, Nefer'Kemnebit, felt almost ill at ease.

Without thought she threw a small, silent curse at the Mad Ones for the poor timing, but she had no choice now: she had to offer her Sire, the Elvern supreme ruler Watchéran, obedience and honour before seeking out her Mama and though He appeared not to have seen her yet, protocol - *and thereby her Mama* - would most assuredly not allow her to slight him.

Masking the streak of impatience that ruled on the inside, but portraying nothing but serene calm, she changed direction, steering towards the temporary canopy of scarlet cloth that screened He-who-is and his visitor from the heated kiss of the scorching sun. Regally plush, the royal awning offered an impressive splash of both shelter and colour amidst the sun-drenched courtyard - and if from afar it looked nothing much, she already knew it would measure a good twenty paces from corner to corner, for she'd seen it erected oft enough.

Playing down an itch above her right ear, she acknowledged that on any other day, she might have relished the prospect of its shelter, but today she was preoccupied and the relentless mass of red amongst the gleaming buildings, only served to bring the crux of her vision back. Determined to keep the issue personal though, she steeled herself but didn't quite manage to banish the notion. With the complete absence of even the finest breeze, the fabric hung unmoving in the morning stillness, too vivid in colour, and as she approached she was repeatedly reminded of the blood on the betrayed woman already dead before she touched the ground.

Nefer swallowed bile, for a blink seeing someone else's blood-drenched hands in place of hers and though she knew it childish, she rapidly looked down her pristine pleats, also fearing that just like the woman of the chestnut hair in her vision, she too might see her clothes ruined by a sister's precious lifeblood.

There was nothing to see of course, yet the grief-remembered swelled. She'd tried to save her twin... *No, not her*, she told herself firmly, *but the woman with the chestnut hair had tried. The Mshai had irrevocably betrayed her though; had betrayed them both, and she'd been too late to make a difference. Too late...*

A sense of foreboding filled her and for a blink her arm throbbed again, but it wasn't real. *Not yet.*

She had to find her Mama and petition the Council. *She had to!* This was just a quick stop on the way - and though it delayed her, the Watchéran should be honoured by his own blood.

She deliberately lengthened her strides. She was nearly there now. *The Watchéran, He-Who-Is, looked to be busy; this wouldn't take long. Just quickly bow and be away, now. Just as usual.*

Eyeing the two ever-present, black-skinned Mkhai as she drew closer to the canopy, she marvelled at their ability to stand ever-immobile a perfect five paces from He-Who-Is as though they had an inner connection alerting them to the exact presence of her Sire at any given time.

*Well perhaps they did,* she mused. Both the guards belonged to the elite phalange of personal fighters protecting He-Who-Is and they held themselves with such a perfect stillness that were it not for the shallow rise and fall of their chests, they could have been a pair of full-sized statues carved from flinty obsidian. Never would she make the mistake of thinking them passive though, for they were deadly. Once, one such black-skinned Mkhai had thrown his golden sefret blade with such force that it had cleanly severed an assassin's head from his body.

It had been a frightening experience. She'd been thirty-two, maybe thirty-three, and she'd never seen it coming. The servant assassin had been an eviscerating shadow – one amongst many – and then...

The Mkhai's reaction had been unerring: an instant response to a barely-seen threat that had found the perpetrator dead before he'd even lifted the poisonous blade intended for the heart of his target.

Of course, He-Who-Is had simply laughed in the face of the danger averted and had then proceeded to honour the vigilant guard with a touch and a blessing that had continued to surround the guard to this day. *Why her sire could simply laugh at something so terrifying, she'd never understood but then again, why not?* After all, she reflected, as a living God, earth, water and sky bent to the Watchéran's Persuasions, perhaps even Time – why should He not simply laugh, when there was so precious little to fear from his mortal subjects?

But that was all a very long time in the past now and today no assassins lurked and all was quiet. The two Mkhai on guard, knew her on sight, of course: she'd have no cause for alarm from them, and still…

*Did she not just feel a quiver of intimidation as she walked towards them?!*

Sure, for the moment, their golden sickle swords sat sheathed peacefully whilst their badges of honour, the mottled skins of yellow mountain leopards, hung smartly across their hips atop draping knee-length kilts of black- and cloth-of-gold. And sure, quite unlike anyone else around the Complex they appeared to utterly ignore her, but she wasn't fooled: they might not be men born with the Affinity for sorcery nor were they capable of manipulating their Inner Sight as she were, yet she knew that they *saw* everything regardless. *They would acknowledge only her Sire though for their eyes and lives were for Him - and not even the Best-Loved Daughter could sway their gaze as she drew past.*

She halted her approach as were proper, shifting her gaze to study her father and his visitor surreptitiously where they lounged in the pink-cast shade on lion-footed divans. Interestingly, a third divan stood abandoned in their midst whilst a veritable feast awaited, untouched, on the low table between the two.

With just a tiny bit of effort, she ignored the tasty looking pieces of ice-chilled mango as she gracefully sank to her knees, crossing her arms over the chest and lowering her head briefly. Before He-Who-Is, her father Sheshem'Kufunar – God and Founder of the Living Lands of the Sabén-Heshep – not even Nefer would dare presume enough familiarity to remain on her feet; indeed, not even if the two men before her looked to be fast riveted in serious conversation without an eye to spare for their surroundings.

In spite the nuisance of her detour, her Sire drew her eye as always when she shared His presence. Clear-eyed and hard of long muscle, His black skin shone with the ever-alluring bluish-hue that was common for most Elvern of the Sabén-Heshep, but the Watchéran could never be like anyone else. Not truly. And if Sheshem'Kufunar was no longer entirely in his youth, he was the Esteemed Watchéran of the Sabén-Heshep people nevertheless. Their health shone from her father like an invisible aura, offering Him the look and strength of a man still in his prime. Relaxed yet attentive to his visitor, he reclined easily in his seat amongst a number of brightly-tasselled cushions, and suddenly she couldn't begrudge the delay after all and she found herself only pleased he looked healthy.

Awe and love followed: it was in her blood; in what was owed. This close she felt it like a compulsion and it was right. *To be near He-Who-Is, was quite simply to be near Power; near Life. How could anyone not want that?*

A sudden ease enveloped her and she shifted her gaze.

A quick peek towards the elderly man facing her father from across the table of mother-of-pearl inlay and sumptuous food, failed to identify him as anyone already familiar to her but this came hardly as a surprise. Amongst others, nobility, petitioners and ambassadors came to see her Sire in a never-ending stream of visitors to the Royal Complex - and failure to recognise the face of one older man was understandable.

Still, his presence was arresting though: understated and calm, but unmistakably Elvern and, if she was not mistaken, someone of Power too, and-

Nefer felt her eyes widen. *And... and he was a half-ling too, now that she looked closely!*

It jolted her and curiosity unfurled. The older man's gaze - firm and open – showed her a set of Human eyes: startlingly Elvern blue, iridescent yes - but the black pupils as round and as small as pin-heads in the sharp light!

This most definitely made her father's visitor a 'half-breed'; a *'Nefer-Senef'* amongst the Sabén-Heshep, and - according to the Elder Scrolls - something unspeakable in the Sabén-Heshep former home of Heirah-Noor. Here in their new lands, it was not such an unusual thing of course, but neither was it a particularly common sight within the intimate circle of her father's inner court. *Would his teeth be Human or Elvern...?*

Fascinated, the girl stopped herself from staring outright but her gaze lingered unobtrusively all the same. The guest's wrists were adorned by a set of powerful benedictions that flashed golden and silver as he gestured, and they were intricate; of a kind she'd never before seen. It further peaked her intrigue. *Perhaps the guest was from the provinces?* You could usually tell a person's rank and heritage from the number of painted benedictions and protections they wore, but she could not see enough on this man to stable him with the usual nobility. As it were though, two wrist markings hardly warranted that much respect. *And yet he was here: in private audience with her Sire. A stranger... but not a stranger.*

37

She watched the guest talking to her Sire in muted, insistent tones, and his behaviour soon led her to understand that he was not just another random head-of-state. Her father wore no regalia today - *no crown or state pectoral* - and indeed, had it not been for the presence of the wide serpentine ring cinched around His upper arm to symbolise Life's flow across the Living Land, her Sire's status would have remained obscure, but that was in fact considered the opposite of slight.

The girl pursed her lips for a short breath, a frugal pensive mien shifting her features.

Ordinarily, her Sire would only relinquish His rights to wear official regalia when in the presence of a Spell-Weaver and then only when they heralded from the highest order of the 7th Tier. *It didn't happen often.* Amongst the Elvern of Sabén-Heshep, there were now only fifty Weavers alive to claim such Affinity and she knew them all by sight. This Nefer-Senef was not amongst them and it surprised her to see her Sire so humble.

It made her itch to blurt out a question to satisfy her own curiosity but as of yet, both men still failed to note her presence so she followed protocol, patient like the fishing Heron, awaiting her Sire's pleasure now.

It would be a hot day yet, she decided, semi-distracted just a little by the iced-mango on the mother-of-pearl table. *Hot... yes...*

Her mind wandered but she pushed to clear off the sensation. Even under the awning, the air was warm if not yet stifling, but as she knelt there at least she caught the benefit of her Sire's gracious serving girls as they gently produced a small ripple of air by manipulating two large ostrich-feather fans on ten-foot canes. It felt wonderful against the day's rapidly building heat and for a moment, she forced herself to quietly enjoy this small respite. Even if she failed to relax completely, the sound of her Sire's low voice and his guest's occasional word of agreement, continuously helped cement her in the mundane 'now' where her visions had no power to threaten her. And it was a mercy.

She exhaled silently and enjoyed the hazy, pretty rosy tint to the floor, feeling the monotony stretch and buckle till her eyes began to droop.

*Reality flickered.* With a jolt of alarm, she fought it, but her best effort was not quite enough. *Without further warning, vision tumbled in: filling her, clouding her awareness, pulling her down...*

Impossibly, she had a moment's wherewithal to comprehend that visions of this magnitude had only ever claimed her so completely with the aid of the spelled crystals to focus her mind but then the knowledge was whisked from her like a bad spirit swooping in from the Void to steal her soul. For a split heartbeat longer her physical vision flickered - her mind in chaos, refusing to marry up the picture before her with the one seen within: grasslands and sword-song warred with the muted voices and the presence of her Sire and His guest. *The awning seemed to billow just once. Red on red.*

Her eyes rolled back in their sockets...

*Through somebody else's eyes; through vision that is blurred and oddly skewed, she hears the subdued, yet undeniably heartbroken sobs of a woman in despair as she rushes across a wide grassy field sown with chaos and bodies, and she takes a moment to realise that the harrowing sounds appear to be emanating from herself. No not her! But from the woman whose eyes she is temporarily 'borrowing'!*

*Coherent thought materialises like a flash but even as it goes through her, the distinction between her and the woman begin to blur. Panicking, she fights it, afraid of losing herself, but the grief in her heart immobilises her, subduing all else. Another sob rakes her. Almost she tumbles to the ground as yet again her multiple gossamer layers of creamy skirts interfere with her strides in spite of the gown being fashionably slashed to mid-thigh on either side. Miraculously, she recovers her steps without falling and stumbles on. She has no time to stop and relieve herself of the cumbersome fabrics; desperately she forces on.*

*She stumbles again. Then runs. Lungs burning, she doesn't even have the breath to curse her own clumsiness - it is not that she is unfit but she is winded from fighting an impossible number of well-trained enemy soldiers; tired beyond reason. Her mount is long gone: ripped from girth to belly by the Venzoian she killed, and since the fall she can't seem to breathe properly.*

*For a heartbeat the hideous sound of her doomed horse haunts her along with the fear of dying as she crashes to the ground amidst a body of scales, thrashing equine hooves, and the slashing claws of a monster revving to gut her.*

*Then that's gone too. Though it should have done, the terrifying event holds no meaning; there is currently no room for that feeling within her - not in the face of what she's witnessed only moments before, engaging the hated creature to win a path through to her twin's side.*

*Her mind flickers to the betrayal but she cannot contain that feeling either because maybe she will just cease to exist then – and she must... she must keep moving. If she does, everything will be right. Everything...*

*And so, for now, she simply runs: ankle paining; lungs burning; sword arm throbbing, all the while praying – yes, praying! -that she's misunderstood; knowing already that she hasn't.*

*From the left, a soldier in foreign colours looms in, clearly with the hope to intercept her. He is followed by a companion-in-arms tight on the heels, and she thinks for a moment that they might have a good chance at succeeding and suppresses despair. The two men are moving fast, for they wear only the same excellent light-armour of chainmail and gambesons as the rest of the enemy men, and they appear to have taken just one look upon her dirt-smeared, tear-stained face before dismissing her ability with the gore-splattered sword she's somehow kept a-hold of. And why not? She knows how she must look to them in torn skirts of fine silk and trailing masses of hair held back now only by the stubborn will of one lingering Dragon Silver comb: a Lady of the Court, crazed with fear.*

*Rather than resorting to relying on his own weapons to take care of her, the first man makes as if to capture her with his arms and her heart leaps. She cannot let them stop her. Wishing for the magic, yet feeling no trace of it, she swings the sword instead. Fainting right... for she has no strength...*

*The weight of the blade feels unspeakably foreign to her; as though made from a metal too heavy for her to lift now, and for a heartbeat she fears that she might drop it when a spasm goes through her injured arm, hindering the move. Fortunately, the aggression is still ripe enough to force the soldier to veer off from the sudden threat and as the second man makes a grasp for her arm, he catches only the fine netting of her sleeve. It tears like paper under his grip, but she grits her teeth against the pain of extra effort and forces her legs to move faster.*

*She just has to make it to the edge; that's all! Has to make it across to where her sister folded to the ground, fluidly - as though someone had chosen that very moment to magically melt every last bone in her body - except that the fountain of blood seen pouring from the cut in her throat tells the story of things less-extravagant.*

*But dear spirits, it cannot be real! Let it not be real!*

*Vaguely she perceives the thwarted soldiers striking up a pursuit, the echoes of their enthusiasm floating on the wind as they egg each other on but the mere threat of them capturing her before she can reach her twin sister, gives her stamina a boost. Awareness grips her that the sword-song has weaned to a sporadic, grating melody now; incidental as more and more of their own soldiers fall or surrender to the hopeless number of enemies and nightmare creatures that stalk the fighters – friend and foe alike - waiting; hungering. Something is holding them back, she knows: otherwise they'd be mindlessly killing by now but this is not her concern. Only her sister…*

*The slash above her left eye where the dying Venzoian has caught her with a slicing kick of freak coincidence now throbs in rhythmic pace with every one of her straining heartbeats and it makes it hard for her to see properly, but it doesn't matter. Little does...*

*For a moment she almost falters as she pictures the horrifying moment where her own husband's handsome sword glints wicked warning in the callous sunlight before he lets it bite into her sister's neck... executing... merciless... hard...*

*Her heart twists. No! She has to be wrong: an illusion of the eye! He is supposed to protect her sister beyond all and everything – not kill her like he would a filthy thief in the night, with one single, economic slash bestowed in disregard of everything they'd been fighting for; of everything he's said and done: of the love she's felt burning her insides with fire and need for such a long time now whenever she's thought of him: whenever he has looked at her, or touched her, or-*

*Her heart curdles as her mental world dissolves in ashes. Why? Wretched, why? How could he? And again her mind baulks: she must be wrong! Has to be!*

*But new panic claws at her. Dear spirits, but she cannot see her sister move. Cannot even really see her form clearly behind the half-a-dozen armed enemy soldiers surrounding the two men she is steering towards: one man so hauntingly familiar – the other an apparent stranger to her eye. And she tries not to notice the two black-scaled Venzoians as they loiter, oddly calm behind the unknown enemy commander.*

*Another twenty paces… she can follow her husband's trail of death to the edge… ignore the Night Crawlers…*

*She can see her beloved and the enemy leader conversing, the latter apparently enjoying himself; her husband palely serene, though his eyes are fiery like magic and his white shirt irrevocably tainted by his horrendous deed…*

*And then… And then she is there!*

*Beyond care, she throws the costly sword to the ground. She does not have the strength - nor the inkling - to fight all these people; all she wants is to see her sister: to tell her that things are going to be fine! As they always are; they'd been in worse and survived…*

*Her arrival causes a stir but she has managed to surprise them enough to shoulder her way between two enemy soldiers before they might think to stop her, and without as much as a single glance for anyone present, she scans the ground, searching…*

*Lack of breath stops her dead. There she is: her sister's still form - just a little to the right of the group she's intruded upon - as though the men have deliberately drifted from the spot; and no wonder. A gasp of pain escapes her like a ripple of madness: the keening song of a lost spirit growing within.*

*After the flurry of activity and violence, she is now suddenly unable to move; or act; or think. Heartbeats go by. Through the haze, she feels her pursuers stumble into the loose circle of men but if halted by the sight of blood that colours the grass, or if they are gestured to desist by the flame-haired enemy-leader, she doesn't care. One step, then another and another. Moving like a sleepwalker, she barely senses anything as she sinks to her knees next to her sister. Too late...*

*And the blood... so much blood.*

*Bereft, she casts her eyes around. Unable to comprehend... just how much blood... but it is everywhere: in the partially trampled meadow-grass; on her dress where she is kneeling, unable to avoid the spread and still be near her twin; on her sister: spilt down the front of the once rose-coloured gown like some freakish accident with a wad of fabric-colourant. On her sister... On her sister... On...*

*On her sister, now pale as a shrine effigy of Silicia'Cha and in death still beautiful as ever. Except for her eyes. Eyes that now stare upon the Void beyond forever with a most bewildered look of surprise in their frozen depths.*

*Reality flickers...*

*Haltingly she puts her shaking hands on her sister's horrifyingly simple wound as though in hope that she might somehow close the gash, but her sister's chest remains more still than a long winter's night.*

*The shaking spreads from her hands to her body then.*

*For one crazy moment she looks inwards for any kind of law-defying, magical Weave to alter the impossible but there is nothing. The spark is gone. One hand leaves her sister's neck to stroke the ever-silken hair as though in comfort.*

*But who's comfort?*

*Of course, her gesture is pointless and as her fingers trail away, her touch only serves to leave a smear of crimson behind, and suddenly her vision is swimming.*

*Too late... so much blood... too late...*

*A keen escapes her again, like a sob - but harder - and suddenly she cannot breathe as she rocks forward over the body, uncaring how the ends of her too-long hair trail through the already-congealing wealth of blood. When she rocks back on her heels in desolate despair, the feathery ends paint delicate, macabre lines across the gold-shimmering bodice of her own once-beautiful gown. They vaguely remind her of brush-strokes... she knows she cannot bear this... panic begins to wilt her ability to think... there has... there has to be something!*

*She looks up but does not let go of her twin. She does not really see anything, not even the breathtaking view presented right before her - a mere five feet away, where the hill-meadow finishes before a drop of chilling proportions.*

*Help! She must find help!*

*She looks over her shoulder to the oddly sombre faces of the men behind her but she does not really see them - or their ready weapons, for that matter - nor does she even really look at her husband, the one who is guilty of betrayal; of murder. For a moment she doesn't care about anything as the pain of losing her sister becomes real.*

*"Help her!" The words leave her mouth without her realising that she's about to speak. The language seems unknown to her and yet she understands her own plea as do the men for they look 'affected': rooted to the ground - unable to help? Unwilling?*

*A spark of anger ignites in the pit of her heart.*

*Louder yet, she demands, "Help her, please! Somebody help her! You must help her!"*

# Lost

*A 'flecking age'? How does one determine what constitutes
a 'flecking age'?*

Solancei did not have a clock to check the actual time; there
was no way of knowing if it mirrored the feelings of her body and
mind - *everything was relative* – but still!

She saluted her smouldering torch with a worried frown. To
be sure, it felt like a 'flecking age', and judging by the less than
optimistic size of the once-roaring flame, she'd most definitely
walked a 'flecking age', yet what did she have to show for the
effort?!

She forced herself to keep alive a sliver of cheer. It was false
sentiment, but sometimes she was almost as good at lying to herself
as Iambre.

Since locking the two muscle hounds away in her former
prison cell, she'd made a 'clean get-away' in as much as nobody
seemed to be following her, and she had to believe it was a good
thing. *Yet still, still, still...*

Well, she must have traversed corridors and climbed a
thousand stairs by now, all without seeing a whiff of daylight, and
with the soft scuff of her own steps the only sound to accompany,
her initial triumph was weaning. *No sounds, no people, no nothing!*
It was not how she'd envisioned this. *Well,* she amended, *at least not
until now. Because now there was a light.*

Again she forced her eyes to scout ahead, determined to stop
herself thinking about the pointless subject of time now that she

finally appeared to be getting somewhere. The steep passage she'd been following was unlit, and yes - it had taken her a flecking age to get this far - but she hoped it had been worth it, because the light she'd spied ahead was the first of its kind. *What did it matter that it was nothing but a simple tapering sliver, filtering out from around what must be yet another relatively poorly-fitting door?* It might not be much, but it was light, bless the Gods. *It was light!*

She pushed at her own weariness and centred on placing one boot before the other. *Up. Up. Up.* With her torch burning lower than low, this had appeared just in time, and if it brought with it a whisper of false hope and futile longing, she'd take it over the darkness. *Take that… and worse.*

Solancei shook off the notion of optimism before it sparked too far beyond control. *This kind of darkness was enough to make a dreamer of anyone, but that was fine; no one ever need know of it. Rats, and who could judge anyway?* This was the first indication that she might be reaching a place of something other than stone and dampness, and it could be good or bad, but as the door ahead was also the first of its kind she'd encountered since the prison cell, she just couldn't stop herself from hoping this would be that long-sought exit.

*Yes, and if you wish it, so it shall be, because luck has ever been so flecking kind to you, hasn't it!?* The caustic sarcasm jagged through her mind without remorse, for knowing her exact luck, this would be but another disappointment more like. *These corridors seemed endless; already the passage of time eluded. What more are you losing track of?! Good sense? Your mind? Gods… and Iambre would be livid by now. Livid and worried!*

Rubbing her brow with her palm, for the twentieth time trying not to think of the implications, Solancei knew there would be trouble ahead on that account. In many ways, the Princess did everything so right: her healthy strength of character, her compassion, her care for diplomacy and law, her idea of sacrifice, but…

But unfortunately, her cousin did not cope well with stress. Like anyone, Iambre had faults, well-hidden to the casual observer but easy to spot for those who truly knew her, which - Gods save them all - kind of made that woman's reaction to things unforeseen just about as certain as the call of Venzaela's Chime, when it tolled precisely twice a day to announce the hour of Noon and Midnight to the citizen of Etruia City. *Predictable. Ever predictable.*

Solancei chewed her cheek in deep-seeded worry, keeping her eyes on the frame of light as her mind curdled. Best not to think about it, but by now Iambre was bound to be in a 'state', and when such a thing occurred, she was wont to do silly things! *Really silly things – as in things that should be prevented!*

Solancei scrunched up her face in thought. Well fine, perhaps she might be exaggerating Iambre's tendencies in her own mind now; perhaps it was not all that bad, and-

*No* - she revised, laying off the cheek as she tasted blood - *actually it was just that bad!* True, on occasion, she herself was not the best person for objectivity but Iambre was spoilt: first, she'd rant. Then she'd fret. And then… *And then she would demand answers!*

50

The roughened wood of the torch digging into her palm, she unclamped her cramping hand, realising then just how tightly she was suddenly gripping the base in response to the nerves that danced without grace along her insides. Klaas had better be clever in her approach, she reflected with hollowing dread; had better be delicate in how she addressed this 'incident' with Iambre. Gods, but should the princess think Solancei's ill-timed absence deliberate, then-

She snapped for air, eating an uncomfortable breath. *Childhood friends or not, Iambre might choose to retaliate against that sort of 'offence' with a strike of her own, and fleck...*

Solancei shivered, fearing the line of her thoughts. *Iambre would use Solancei's 'call of poor judgement' as an excuse to take advantage of the situation with a certain Captain Metavo. Or, - a* small inner voice amended, *- perhaps she was too foolish if she carried a hope that the princess had not already done so?!*

She closed her eyes tightly just a little longer than a blink, wishing this would all end. *Of course Iambre might not react like that at all. Her friend could be very sensible, couldn't she? Perhaps if Klaas was forced to own up? Perhaps if the Chief was pushed to reveal the truth? To explain?*

Solancei winced. One scenario was almost as bad as the next. *Of course, Metavo might manage to rebuff Iambre as he had done on times before, or...*

Solancei felt like she'd swallowed rocks as her stomach clenched. The Gods seemed to have gone out of their ways to spill disaster into her life an obscene number times already – mostly with narrow margins for recovery - and now...?

*And now this! Flecking Simaro!*

She wiped her clammy forehead on a sleeve and sighed, distilling a flash of anger. *Don't think; don't think; don't think! No, do not think about Iambre, nor of the worry you will be causing her no matter Klaas' chosen angle. Do not think of the need for you to get back before the princess turns the entire town upside down in righteous demand that someone finds me! Do. Not. Think.*

Solancei snatched a short meaty breath feeling almost faint with the possibilities of this turning increasingly disastrous before she might successfully extricate herself from the mess. *These tunnels... please... it had been a flecking age! Please, please let that light be enough to fuel more than frayed yearnings. Please...*

With the depth of her own desperation, her optimism wilted yet again.

Simaro wanted to hang her. *What if there was no escape? What if she was destined to wander down here until the torch burned out and her legs gave way?* Those prospects were grim. She could baste her theory with the thickening gravy of darkness and the chilling damp surrounding her; she could let the fear of tomorrow grow and grow till the smell of her mounting despair rose up her backside to strangle her, but such pass time would prove 'a poor pursuit'. *There had to be a way out! Desire and Veranto had to take her through this! It must, for if either gave out...*

Solancei eyed the light with a sceptical smile as it grew a little more wholesome with every step. She'd hate to admit that there was a chance that maybe she'd erred when she made her initial escape, but-

She closed her line of thought down, thinking 'yes', nodding her head mentally 'no'.

Riled up by her own needs she'd followed Simaro for a while after escaping: stalking him like a shade in the wake of his fickle torch-light, yet taking care to stay well-back, hidden in the darkness so that even should he or the men turn, they would fail to notice her.

*But you didn't dare push that famous 'luck' of yours though, did you?* The thought was accusing. *You did not dare stick around, nor trust your own run of fortune. Kira'Cha never loved you like she does Iambre, and don't you know it!*

She flexed her fingers around the torch, feeling the unfinished wood imprint itself on her palm.

There was no point in looking back. Kira'Cha, curse her, would have withdrawn her luck sooner or later - if nothing else, Solancei knew this. *There'd been a hundred things that could've made him think to turn around; a hundred and more…*

She forced down a steady breath. Well damn it, but in truth, she'd wanted to be long gone from him. The sooner, the better! When he learnt of her escape, the hunt would be on, so when they'd passed a fork in the tunnel where another torch sat forlornly lit in a sooty bracer… *well, it had seemed an invitation too obvious to ignore!* She'd wanted distance, had hung back…

She swallowed her doubts as she had done then. Watching Simaro's torch-light wean, then disappear, had been both a relief and a curse, and she'd waited only a blink then before darting forth, leaving the shroud-like protection of darkness behind to snatch the new torch and veer down the alternate branch of tunnel. *It could well still prove a damning mistake.* She knew it now as she'd known it then, and still...

*At the time it hadn't seemed important that the way forward had looked darker than Inkar'Chi's heart; she'd made her escape. She was free.*

Solancei released a reluctant sigh in the murky light. None of that could be helped now; not even if Klaas would surely be yelling at her stupidity when she found out. *It didn't matter.* She'd made a choice. *Klaas was not the one stuck in this mess, so Klaas could stick it!*

That jackal fight had turned everything upside down and you could surely not be at fault if it left you with an overwhelming need to remove yourself from further danger! *In her generous opinion, Simaro was not of a sound mind. He surely was not.*

Face twisting, she recognised her own folly. *Yet again she was trying to raise her own spirits.*

Did she not already know that Klaas would turn a deaf ear to her meagre evasions? Did she not already know that hauling a bunch of feeble excuses before the Chief, with the ambition in mind that she'd react with leniency, never worked? Sadly, in truth, there was no question about how this would play out – and she knew this too. When she got out of here, she feared she stood to face the biggest bollocking of her life: from her mentor, from her Princess, and then-

*It'd be like going from the skirmish into battle.* Fair or not, that was the size of it. She knew because that's how it always was when she messed up. *With the Chief you either succeeded – or you screwed up. It was rousingly simple if little else were.*

Feeling uneasy, Solancei clutched the torch, her fingers sawing on the wood. All she must do now was to carry on! *Carry on as expected - and get herself out of this mess.* Except, yet again she was inspired to think how Klaas was not the one who was uncomfortably warm and cold all at the same time; nor was Klaas the one who'd had to face Simaro's odd idea of justice, or had gotten herself knocked for six when trying to escape a team of fully armed men out to hunt her like a white stag for the king's high table. This was all so far from regular, that she wanted to scream with something that looked like anger, but felt like cold fear. She'd done a lot of odd things in her life so far; some good, some bad, some reckless, some a mix of the above and more - depending on the point of view – but she had never been lost in a dungeon before; had never been injured like this; had never gone against caution to link with the State of Veranto for such an impossible length of time.

She eyed the seductive strip of light, longing flaring and dying, then flaring again. *It was further than she'd thought; her speed was waning, her mind... flexing.* It was disturbing to know she was moving within new, mostly unchartered ground, where her actions thus far had gone grossly against many teachings. For this misconduct, the Enclave might demand her permanently expelled. Or punished. Still, her duty to Iambre must come first. No matter what had gone before, no matter what awaited, she had a responsibility to get herself back to her Charge by any means necessary.

Solancei felt her head spin. Now Klaas being Klaas, might have known how to handle it, whereas she-

*But how could Klaas have let it come to this, though?* For all her scheming and plans and secrecy, was it indeed possible that the Chief had erred?

Solancei smiled with brittle humour at the idea, but the curl of doubt still hooked her, yanking softly at the seams of her cultured regard. Respect was everything: respect and loyalty and trust, and yet it cut both ways. *Chief Eso Mehadja could have done this on purpose. Just to see...*

Bothered by the idea of this possible 'betrayal', she wiped a hand across her face as if she might wipe away more than perspiration, but it brought little true comfort. She felt feverish but in truth the temperature in these tunnels exceeded her former cell by less than a margin for her leathers were still little more than semi-dry, and it left her as uncomfortable as ever, the string chafing her outer thigh and the waistband riding low, forcing her to endure a shift in the tailoring that was not ideal.

As she had also done a handful of times over, she endeavoured to suppress every ill-feeling behind the serenity of Veranto, but she could barely wait to be outside again: could not wait to smell the fresh air; could not wait to sink herself into a hot bath. She wanted tempered wine and white chicken; indeed, the prospect of a lengthy Kizano session did not seem at all that unattractive right then either – anything, as long she was far away from this place. *Any. Flecking. Thing!*

Impatient desire washed over her, pushed by a little panic. *This entire thing – the fight, the capture, the cell, her tricking the two jailers in best Ina Uttorian style… it was all ludicrous!* By necessity this would cost her! Even submerged in the State of Veranto, this constant level of exercise was draining and she'd already been abusing her skills beyond normal application. Sooner or later there would be backlash; she needed proper medical assistance; the quicker she was able to relinquish her dependence, the better, and-

Well Gods, the Veranto could glitch at any moment, and then what? What if she blinked or accidentally lost focus and it escaped her grasp? *What then?* At some point she must relinquish the Link; at some point she must square up to suffer the consequences of her 'abuse', but what was her time frame?

Solancei trembled with sour, reversed anticipation. The light was so close now. That and escape was all that mattered, yet somewhere deep she also hoped that Klaas had not done this to her on purpose. *She really, really hoped!*

Again she looked at the flame rising from her torch. *Was it a little less bright? Was it a little smaller than last time she'd looked?*
*Maybe.*

She drew a cleansing breath, but something within resisted; her throat felt raw; it made her focus waver. *Just a few more steps. Just…*

Forcing her mind to think about the possibility of an encounter soon, she tried to summon rightful concern, but thus far she'd seen no other living creature down here and the presence of a single door seemed unlikely to alter this: a fact not just brazenly assumed, because after coming across a handful of identical chambers left long-cold, all littered with broken bits of furniture, reeking of stale air and seasons of abandonment, Solancei just didn't really believe that she'd find anyone beyond this door either. Most of the other 'rooms' had been left randomly open, some of them with half-rotten doors hanging off rusty hinges that would creak as she pushed her way past, ambushed by smells of dank, decaying wood. *Gods, yes even the rats seemed to shun the place, so as for people...*

Slowing right down to approach the door, she lowered the stinking torch; heart beating like a hammer on an anvil, she crept closer. The snifter of light was a blessing, but she could hear her own breaths and was only partly successful in silencing them - the exertion of rapidly climbing the staircase having been too extreme for her current health.

*Too loud. She was surely too loud?!*

She crouched and absent-mindedly touched the broad, functional hilt of the bull seax secured by her bootstraps to the outside of her right shin. It was an uncomfortable place to keep it but she resisted the urge to free the knife. She could feel herself shaking from buried fatigue and didn't trust that she wouldn't drop the blade: a noise that surely would give her away, should there be anyone present behind that door after all. *Caution. She must remain cautious!*

With the echoes of her own subdued breath sounding louder than possible in the still, musty air, Solancei put an ear to the door. Iambre was on her mind - *how could she not be?* - but she could not afford to worry about her friend right now, nor about her friend's

58

questionable ability to stay aloof when Metavo was near. If this mess hadn't happened, Solancei could've been back in time to assure that Iambre kept it all above board with the Captain on that first night in Zanzier: she could've-

She slammed a mental fist down on the *what-ifs*. Her thoughts were moths fluttering chaotically around a forgotten lantern at night, breaking themselves against the glass panes – bruising her wings of serenity, costing her coins of confusion and adversary, but she was done!

Ignoring a light-headed sensation, she tried to realign purpose with caution. If anyone was behind this door, she couldn't tell and with a sudden strain of impatience, a rise in apathy rendered her suddenly bold with indifference to the potential danger... *Gods, but if Iambre had forgiven Captain Metavo...* not a single sound met her from within... *If she had forgiven him, then-*

Snarling at her own lack of discipline, Solancei snatched the hasp, simultaneously curling her fingers abruptly around the wonky metal latch to plummet forward.

A blaze of warmth and light hit her like a wall, followed in a flash by relief and disappointment both. Just like everywhere else she'd tread, the room revealed itself empty of life, yet quite *unlike* any of the other dank rooms she'd crossed, this one was most definitely still in use!

For a handful of beats she remained perfectly still, a bout of excitement flattening her previous emotions. A stout table - clean-scoured and functional - along with eight identical chairs, bore witness to the indisputable fact that this guard station might actually still take up some kind of function, and there was very much no evidence of decay. As further evidence, two peat-topped braziers threw out pleasant heat, whilst half-a-dozen wall sconces were responsible for a soft yellow brightness that just exactly failed to cut her eyes. *It felt... civilised. One step removed from hope; one step closer to escape.*

Feeling dazed, she kicked closed the door with the side of her heel, and it obliged by settling back against its misshapen jamb with a soft click as the old latch caught and held. The cordial rise in temperature felt bewitching, her body recalling the gratifying idea of comforts belonging to another world - and without means to stop it, she found herself swaying towards the heat source, the weariness within her doubling to match the new burst of relief that enveloped her spirit. *After the cold tunnels, it was almost too hard to resist. Too hard...*

No longer in need of it, she threw down her near-spent torch. It extinguished itself in a brief flutter of embers but she paid it scant mind as she drew towards the nearest brazier, barely stopping herself from realising the urge to bury both fists deep within the lit bowl. *Mercy... had she really been so cold?* Her entire body seemed to sag as it welcomed the heat like the embrace of a trusted lover, sending a prickling buzz of life down her extremities as her fingers seemed to thaw.

Leaning against the high back of one of the stout chairs, she sighed aloud and fought against the next urge that bid her sit down a while. The warmth was near-overwhelming, dulling her slowing senses as though someone had wrapped her in a cotton blanket and plied her with herbal tea to relax away the stresses of a bleak day. It invited her to close her eyes; to rest, if only for a short while, and she could not have said she minded the idea: this was real and the warmth seemed to sieve right into her skin and bones raising notions of bliss. *Comfort… such plain comfort.*

Without thinking, she flexed the fingers of her right hand and felt the tendons protest. *Veranto or no, the digits still felt stiff and tomorrow her hand would ache for sure.*

Within her, the State of Veranto flickered unsteadily then - like the flame of a candle left in a draughty windowsill, exposed to fine spells of air from without – and the sensation snatched her back to the present as the stabbing fear of losing the Link shot pins up her spine and down her arms. She wanted to stay warm but the small twist of suppressed pain gliding upwards along her ribs warned her just how dangerous a slip might be. *Lose yourself and lose the Veranto – simple…*

Solancei forced her eyes to focus on the brazier's smouldering contents. *This was not safety. Not yet.* The illusion to believe it otherwise was tempting, but the knot of apprehension was back in the pit of her belly, as was the worry what would happen if she gave in.

She felt her throat work and realised she was parched enough to feel the detrimental effects that the lack of fluids would cause, whether the Link shield or not. *It might explain her sluggish head too. But then again, so might the last couple of days!*

Anxious to keep her mind sharp, she forced herself to look around the room then: to the opening in the wall across from her –

*the only exit* – but mercifully lit by sporadic torches leading away into the empty gloom.

*Her vision blurred and she squeezed her fingers tightly around the chair's solid top rail.* The plain, semi-worn wood felt tough to the touch: as though it might gift her with a splinter in the thumb if she was not careful and she focused on that sensation as her eyes drifted from the chair, lengthways across the surface of the unremarkable rectangular plank table.

The sight of the plain earthenware jug that stood besieged by upended stubby cups at the far end, surprised her. For a few breaths she simply stared at the unlikely feature, somehow not connecting it with her needs. Then her heart jolted as thoughts realigned. *An earthenware jug! Which might mean-*

Excitement rolled over her like a slow rush of air, rattling her emotions as though still an Adept. *She wasn't imagining this. It was there.* One rather unassuming clay jug with matching cups, positioned down the far end of the rustic table, closer to one corner than the other, as though whoever had left it, had not placed much importance in the task.

Solancei swallowed, suddenly painfully reminded of a multitude of small necessities. Her mouth had gone as dry as cinders and the near-unquenchable thirst she'd been steadily suppressing, reasserted itself like one of the persistent headaches that normally benched her for hours. Water would be sweet, but right about now she'd settle for any liquid - even the concoction some home-brewers had named 'fox piss', allegedly on account that it was pungent enough to raise the interest of a blind dog, but also pretty undrinkable.

With shaking hands, she pushed herself slowly away from the chair. She felt like a sleepwalker must do: able to move, and perhaps even see too, but everything fluctuated within a strange spectrum where nothing seemed quite solid. *How had she not seen the tray the instant she came in? It held no consequence.* Slowly circling the old trestle, it seemed almost too good to be true. Like with the strange dreams of deja-vu of Iambre and del'Draventar, she felt trapped, unable to move but in one direction, yet fearing that she already knew what would come. The jug would be empty. A trap would spring: like an ambush. Simaro would string her up by the neck, and-

*Nothing happened.* She shook her head. *Mercy, you're losing it!*

Grabbing the jug with a soft prayer, her fingers spasmed twice, offering trouble as she dragged it haltingly towards her, somehow not quite able to concentrate on the effort it would be to physically lift the thing.

With bated breath, she peered over the rim…

# Something Almost Remembered

A hiss of harsh relief escaped her, but for a moment she was rendered too weak to care.

The jug was nearly half full, the murky-looking liquid within as 'innocent' to the eye as usquebaugh – but of a bouquet to the nose that inspired an idea of wine.

With a lurch that made the liquid slush invitingly, she paused just long enough to give the contents a second quick sniff. *And mercy… it was good! No badger's piss, or bat's piss or fox's piss – or whatever else they named those illegal brews of brandy – at worst it might be a watered-down concentrate, at best it might be white apple wine…*

Solancei let caution fly. Temptation pushed her past care.

Too keen to alleviate her thirst, she disposed of decorum, drinking without ceremony straight from the rim that felt thicker than the edge of her thumb. It was not crystal glass, for sure, and in another flash it went through her that everyone she knew, or had ever known, would've been horrified to observe her behave like a common tavern strumpet, but the thought disintegrated. It also didn't matter; her unladylike thoughts about 'Fox Piss' might have provoked similar reactions!

*She would have found it funny, had she cared* – and she drank, what appeared to be diluted wine, in large needy gulps, not bothered that it was weak and tasted of sour grapes and cheap origins.

Returning the jug to the table with an unsteady sway and a new feeling of fiery warmth speeding through her belly, Solancei swung her attention toward the new tunnel, forcing her eyes to focus as she centred on the opening. The path looked level, just about as rough-hewn and pitted as the passages she'd travelled down already, but ultimately more inviting due to the presence of light. It threatened the return of people, true – yet it also lent credit to the intriguing idea of a true way out, and a stab of optimism made her heart flutter as hope danced a new jig. The thin wine had not been nice but it had served to give her an infusion. *New energy solidifying her purpose, as much as she'd have liked to, she could not stay in this room. Iambre… Simaro… Klaas…*

She forced herself to shift; to move; to deliberately let go of the idea of rest. The State of Veranto cupped her and gave her the means to continue: the stamina to press forward and focus. It was ill-advised, and dangerous, and-

*And blah, blah, blah! Klaas was not here!*

Solancei knew the bravado was forced, though. A still, chilly sort of reluctance grated through her to whisper of the truth, but torches led the way now. The pitch on their crowns was liberal: thick enough for a heavy flame to lick the walls like they appeared to have done countless times before, quite as if it was the beginning of the night, not the end, and if the air was a little heavy with the ensuing smoke it was not bad enough to be cloying.

She smoothed wisps of escaped hair back and drew a careful breath. *A bath… soon…*

65

With a tiny smile for the fancy, she walked on. Unsurprisingly, the trajectory soon steepened, the elevation growing ever more pronounced before it finally produced a new set of wide, but shallow stairs. She'd climbed so many steps by now, and yet the sight of stairs charged her with a spark. The torches continued to be regularly spaced. So far she'd met no one. *Kira'Cha, dear, sweet Goddess: we share no love, but perhaps just this once…?*

A little while longer, and nothing changed, then the stairwell began to bend one way then the other on a path that was suddenly becoming visibly different from earlier: broader, but definitely following a bend on a rising incline. *It puzzled; she couldn't make sense of the track – it seemed an impossible trajectory, and to find herself still underground…?*

Slowly the torches became fewer as the gradient increased and the stairs failed to adjust. It made for an unnerving climb – and her imagination soon had Simaro appear several times in front of her: he and his men roving around the next spiralling bend as if he knew of her ascent and was not surprised, whilst she-

It was foolish. Realistically she knew that the sounds of boots and weaponry would've given the man away and there was no sound to proclaim such a possibility. *Was she nearing the surface, though? At what point would she have to be clever to avoid discovery? The 'flecking age' had long since been replaced with a notion of a 'never-flecking-ending-age', but where could she go, but forward?*

To pass the time, she started counting the steps, starting over every time she hit forty – not because she wasn't able to count any higher, but because it made her keep to the illusion that she'd only just set out. She was tiring faster than before, however; if someone was to chance upon her, she'd be slower to react than a hibernating insect, yet with a streak of her usual sardonic practicality, she reasoned that if the worst should come to a crunch, she'd at least have surprise on her side - and, of course, that old seax as well. *The long knife had cut that horny idiot back in the cell well enough* - it would serve – *thirty-eight, thirty-nine, forty!* Solancei puffed her cheeks out. *One, two, three...*

Gods be good, why had that bastard Simaro put her so deep below ground in the first place? It seemed an excessive act. *Another sigh.* It was a bad habit: a dead giveaway that her brief burst of energy was wearing off!

Blowing out her cheeks, she chanced a brief pause to catch her breath. It was not wise, but neither was faltering before she could reach the top.

Leaning back carefully against a deep groove in the wall, she relaxed. Her mind was heavy and rather than fight it, she braced an arm against her injured side and let her head sink slowly to rest against the wall. A deep breath followed and she squeezed her eyes shut for one brief beat of the heart, stupidly wishing that they would have stopped burning by the time she opened them again. Gods help her, but the air felt arid in her lungs, and her throat burned; without the Veranto she would've sunk to her knees or worse, for the weariness had more stamina than she now. *She should never have left Simaro's trail! Never! She could have followed him to the top back when she'd had the chance. Should've; could've; didn't!*

Solancei grimaced with morbid humour and hissed a curse under her breath when a glitch in the Veranto made her eyes fly open as a twinge flickered across her injured ribs. Looking down without really seeing, she laboured to peel herself back off the wall - and there was the thing with monumental tasks... *they were never easy now, were they!?*

She almost managed success. Only her feet did not seem to comply and as she stumbled, forced to brace her arm against the wall or else go flat down, a sobering feeling came over her. *You need food, water, and healing – any order would do. Any order – or...*

Hanging her head, she panted: spent and assailed by a stab of hunger - but it was not as pervasive as the burrowing fatigue. From the corner of her eye, the wall seemed to shimmer, a sure sign that her eyes were giving in to fatigue also. *Or maybe it had been that wine?* Her belly felt slightly unsettled.

Solancei blinked but her eyes blurred in the warm atmosphere. They stung as though the air was heavy with smoke, but it was not, and she couldn't seem to focus; Veranto or not, her mind was dulling; in a beat or two, she'd be on the floor, and she did not rate her chances of getting back up.

Determined for that not to happen, she fought gravity, pushing herself up and forward when a new sparkle on the wall caught her eye. *A tiny square...?*

Mildly charmed she looked towards it and saw it twinkle again. *Not a trick of the eye, then.*

Suddenly intrigued she shuffled a little for a closer look. Senses muted, she briefly wondered if she'd happened upon a half-exposed vein of quartz, but the glittering green spark was too uniform; too square; and as she reached out to brush an experimental finger against it, a spurt of surprise made her look twice, for the surface was smooth.

*Which meant not indigenous, but...? But man-made? Perhaps like a mosaic tile?*

Struck by strangeness, she looked away in slewed thought, her eyes randomly wandering to catch another spark. *Another tile?*

Blinking myopically, she adjusted her eyes to find it so, this one barely a few feet further on from the first. *It was a tile.* Her brow creased with question. She looked away but the two small squares of iridescent green never moved - and as she shifted a little then, changing her line of view, the fall of light revealed to her yet another two tiles, this time a little further on, closely followed by another four.

Solancei cocked her head, the fatigue receding. A quick scout showed her the tiles were multiplying ahead, suddenly dotted randomly along the lower parts of the wall, tantalising like a conundrum.

A sliver of bewildered amazement pushed her mind further back into the present. It made little sense. The small pieces of glass brought her in mind of trinkets lost in a sea of grey, yet from singular appearances, the ones ahead were linking in pairs, forming tiny islands of two or even four, though still randomly placed in relation to each other.

Inspired by mild mystery, admiring the iridescent shine where it caught the torchlight just right and broke the dark with a festive twinkle, she let her gaze follow their flow.

It left her face tinkering with a lop-sided smile for the wonder of this odd display; she couldn't think why anyone had bothered to create this down here. Yet the tiles were all of a shape, all of a uniform appearance, and all roughly of the size of a child's thumbnail - there really could be no question that they formed an odd kind of decoration, but why?

Frown returning, her smile wilted. There was just enough distraction here to overrule the weariness of her body and mind, so she used it, pushed off the wall and began to follow the curving corridor once more, this time focusing her gaze forward to spot new tiles as though in a game. And there were more. So many more... *single... double...* the tiles blossomed as the wall bent, leading the eye into small clusters, which spread like splotches of exotic fruit squashed against the rock, expanding into larger clusters, like the overgrown heads of meadow flowers from a tale of the unbelievable.

*They drew her on.* Somehow, now that she'd spotted them, it seemed she couldn't help but look; a few paces more, and the trail of tiles began to multiply exponentially, linking up with other splotches and patterns through spirals of single or double lines formed out of rows to create several abstract forms. *It was strangely beautiful. It seemed so natural; like the eye just wanted to follow the development. Simple, but complex, amazing and...*

Solancei did not recall herself submitting to it but soon she was craning her neck to follow the geometric circles as they flowed from the walls onto the ceiling and back again. It was impossible to decide where to look next, the eye glided, sticking to the sudden, aggressive swell of colour as the tiles began joining with featured patterns from the opposite wall, only then to veer back around themselves to become part, yet again, of the thicker line and form of other designs. It distracted her further from her tired body, and all the time, more mosaics were added until the tunnel lost the semblance of drab and began resembling a rather fine tapestry. *Who would have made such a thing? Spent the time? Carted the materials? Designed the pictures?* The ornamental attention to detail was fit for the Queen's own chambers and yet the complexity of the patterns made it hard to concentrate on the possibility. The order of tiles was not uselessly random, something within the swirls seemed too hard for her to absorb; she'd need to stop to glean a better look-

*No!*

The single word echoed as if she'd spoken aloud and Solancei felt her mind spin just once, then it seemed to break into pieces and grow still.

She felt cold. The designs were hypnotising; captivating; the colours beneath the light of torches too sharp, and too soft, and too alive. She had not realised how demanding they'd become and to counter the feeling she shook her head. *When had the corridor gone foggy? Her eyes were swimming again...*

A creeping sense of concern wove itself past the gossamer clouds, spiking past the layers of fascination she seemed to have built up around the mosaics, and she jumped a little within her own skin to realise herself suddenly immobile: gaping like a half-wit at the

71

hand that seemed to have trouble lifting up off the tiles she'd placed her palm against.

*You are like a glutton who's revelled in a feast,* she thought to herself as her eyes roved, impressions and ideas still building and filling her with a need to ignore the hand, *soon you will have had too much but by then it'll be too late, you'll be lost in the patterns! Lost...*

The thought struck a chord and for some reason, she was abruptly reminded of being lost in a maze. Ivanor had one sunk into the ground, with five-foot walls of snow and ice, and fantastical carvings out of rock and aquamarine ice to help show the way if you knew where to look; similarly, Servangar also had a maze, but fashioned of bushy trees grown so tall that the runs within lay in permanent shade which in turn had forced the marble plinths to be deliberately raised, so to lift the carvings of various Gods and Goddesses back into the light. In either maze there were no bewildering-complex, geometric patterns, of course, but the mind could get turned around and trapped just as easily as her eyes and mind seem to have become trapped in this puzzle - only in this one, certain impression warned, that here was not a maze designed for the explorer to find their way back out!

The realisation shocked her and in the blink between blinks as fogs cleared from her mind, she saw past the soft illusion and caught a notion of chaos in the way the tiles seemed to caper all around her as though pulsing with life. Without reason, the sight frightened her and she ripped her hand from the wall and walked on faster than before then - concerned now to note how easily her eyes seemed to catch this swirl or that, to be instantly drawn from thought or body if she allowed it.

Eerie feelings ruling her, she walked on. *Just walk. Don't look at any one place for too long. Just walk.* But the patterns were so intricate; how could one not admire them? It seemed criminal. At some point, blues and reds were introduced too, making the odd angles and smooth circles seem positively huge in the flickering torchlight, and still the swell of tiles continued to increase: underfoot, overhead, at the corner of her eye.

Tens, then hundreds, perhaps thousands – the patterns grew, undulating and expanding, filling the rough-hewn walls to bring ceiling and floor into one, now almost closing the gaps of raw wall to make her feel like she'd been swallowed into the bejewelled belly of a leviathan.

It was obscene. Solancei closed her eyes every time she passed a torch. *Meandering madness traipsed at her heels; a never-ending labyrinth of colour and form waited like camouflaged wraiths to reach for her spirit, and if caught…*

Solancei opened her eyes and realised they were already open. She'd stopped in the middle of the corridor, her gaze plastered onto a particular burst of colour with a spiral of mosaic working outwards from a centre point only to twist into five separate strains that went each their individual way: up, down, across the floor…

*Should I go back?* The idea beckoned. *I could go back; not all the way but just until I re-discover the first purple tile-*

She blinked the tears from her eyes. Surprise followed. *It hurt to do so. She should go back; find the purple tile. The very first one...*

But she was too tired and her mind baulked. At the centre of something she'd once known – or maybe she did not yet know it? – there was something that told her not to be tricked. A feeling that she was being influenced and with it came a sneaking sense of the supernatural.

Bewildered, she shook her head, gathering her mind through the Veranto. *She did not want to go back! She was looking for a way out! Why would she go back? Something was not right! How far had she walked since that first tile caught her eye? Forever? A week? A good long, flecking age?*

She looked around with a shiver. Really looked. *Insects climbed her skin - or at least it felt like it - though nothing could be seen.*

It stopped. A stillness void of life followed. The mosaics surrounded her like gems and precious stones, encasing her on all sides like the sequins on one of Iambre's exotic dresses. They drew her mind and eye; they could not be escaped, and yet they seemed to have lost their allure all of a sudden, quite as if someone had pulled away a glittering curtain to reveal all the unknown flaws in a painting she had once found perfect. *It was still an example of remarkable artistry - but it was no longer divine...*

Feeling peculiar suddenly, Solancei shook herself. How easy it would be for a tired mind to relent and get trapped in wonder whilst staring at the designs without hunger for anything else; how easy – she'd almost not realised.

She deliberately stepped to the middle of the corridor then, so as to prevent herself from touching either side even if she should feel the urge, but her head seemed fine now that her purpose was resolved and a childlike relief welled up. Some of the patterns still called to her; she experienced that most disruptive feeling several times more as she pressed on, but it was no longer strong enough to waylay her as it had done to begin with, and she was grateful.

*Somehow there is power here; power that you could use,* her mind sang, but such a thing made no sense and pushing at the feeling, she walked on, closing her senses to the intrigue and temptation that laid siege.

In its place she noticed other things now. Like how the air felt heavy and hot against the parts of her skin that were exposed and that there was a smell of something she'd not been aware of till now; something… *something abrasive to the nose. And when had it become so hot?*

Solancei wiped perspiration from her forehead. All around her the mosaics swam with colour; she was pretty sure the heat had not been part of it before and to make worse the feeling, it seemed to be intensifying with every pace, sending a droll stab of nostalgia through her for the many summers spent by the shores of Lake Etruia.

The fact was that the Province of Etruia could be sweltering in mid-summer and when the sun rose to its fullest in the cloud-free sky, there was little the Etruians could do. The rich retreated for a

75

few months to their villas in the mountains leaving the city curiously quiet, whilst the less fortunate embraced the hot clime and their darkening skin-tones with grace.

As one of the royal family, Solancei had always been obliged to follow the strict tradition of the inner circle, whereby they would remain in residence for one full turn of the moon before likewise retreating. It was to show solidarity with their subjects' plight; how it had always been. Of course, her own origins meant that her skin did not turn as golden as most Etruians - in fact, every year the Queen would frown and mutter words of regret underneath her breath that the Tarléonin clime had irreversibly ruined Solancei's chances of a healthy complexion - and every time, Ishjah's casual grief sent Solancei into a spiral of questions.

Ingrown habit saw her grimace for that particular memory. *If Ishjah did not like her appearances in the best of circumstances, the Queen would shudder in disgust if she could only see her now. Shudder and worse...*

Solancei swallowed this strange sense of homesick longing, feeling pallid both within and out. *In Etruia, a breeze of warm air would be the norm, but here...*

A chilling kind of apprehension rolled within her, thinning her resolve. *Why was it that in here everything seemed wrong? Utterly, utterly wrong! Since arriving in Zanzier, life had become a disaster! A disaster, spearheaded by Simaro!*

Aware that the Veranto might be playing tricks with her after her recent 'afflictions' and 'glitches' – *after embracing the link for so long!* - she took a moment to smooth back her hair and gather her mind. *Peace! She needed to keep the peace within! It was entirely possible that she might just be imagining things here; that she might be hallucinating...*

Breathing in the warm air through her nose, nothing seemed like a trick of the mind, however - and in spite the strange churnings in her belly, she was glad now of the diluted wine she'd pilfered earlier. The mosaic was beckoning and the air was furnace hot; surely it could not just be her imagination.

With a little stab of unease, she forced her feet onwards, normal pace now. She felt so warm that she would love to have stripped down to her small clothes but she was not even tempted. This new, weird sense of unease made the small hairs on her neck and arms rise up and she couldn't ignore a cold trickle of wrongness down her back in spite the invasive heat. *She wished that she had a cup of Etruian Spring water. She wished...*

The mosaic stairwell was assuredly unbearably warm now, yet something in the air made her shiver as the eerie sensation flexed deeper. The tunnel seemed to press in on all sides; it was odd but sudden instinct warned her that she should simply turn around and-

She gnawed at her lip, never feeling the damage. The seax felt impossibly heavy on her leg and she drew it then, not caring if she was being rash. *The next sweeping bend lay ahead; what if there was an ambush?*

That very thought almost made her turn on the spot; she shivered repeatedly, unable to control it, the fact that she was acting irrationally never really something that occurred to her. Something within her tucked at her: some dormant ninth sense of survival just triggered by an ancient sensation that spelled death in the flow of the air, in the smell, in the taste, but the task seemed too enormous. *She'd come so far...*

Willing herself to move forward was not simple. With every step, the strange chill only deepened, carving straight through the Veranto as though the Link meant nothing.

*Turn and leave,* her instinct bid her, *just turn and leave.*

# Out of Shadows

Coiled in readiness to deal with trouble, Solancei hugged the wall. The bend was losing its curve. Ahead pulsed a golden-orange light like a tired heartbeat, the nuances barely altering, though also not a complete constant. To Solancei the glow felt heavy as weighted air, the intensity too strong to originate from simple torches now, and it made her pause.

It could be light from the castle furnaces, she allowed. *Which might of course also account for the mounting heat...*

A shiver traipsed down her back, but she started forward again. She wasn't aware if Zanzier Castle had similar features to Ivanor; indeed she could not remember seeing any pipes in her allocated chamber, but she supposed a mere handmaiden might not warrant that kind of luxury in accordance with Zanzierian standards.

She grimaced inwardly with derision, but though a plausible idea, it didn't quite ring true; there were no pipes in Iambre's apartments either, nor had she spied any on their group's extensive tour to get settled in - yet the tunnel temperature was certainly baking; soaring now; and definitely of the same calibre as that recalled from childhood. It alleviated a little stress. *Ivanor... freezing above ground, yet criminally hot below... oh, the memories...*

The light undulating, swaying the shadows, moving them... it made her recall the multiple times fascination with hearsay and old stories had found her descending into the fortress' subterranean levels to stand before the giant furnace doors, eager to catch just a glimpse of the fires before her face cooked to the colour of the small tough-skinned tomatoes cultured and carefully ripened in her mother's orangery by meagre summer sun and Taliana's doting attention. She'd usually been spotted before allowed the treat of a look, but then she'd found the vents and three times in as many days, she'd made the climb to wedge herself onto a shelf near the ceiling. The sight of the huge living fire had been worth the discomfort. She'd found the route just a week before her parents' accident. *After the third time, she'd never been back. Then Klaas had come...*

The present corridor straightened. The imaginary ambush averted, Solancei tip-toed on. Ahead the tunnel ran straight for approximately five paces, then turned abruptly left. At the turn the Mosaics came to a sudden uniform end, stripping the tunnel back to plain dark rock once more. As if to make up, the heat grew like a pulse speeding up, the mystic light deepening and lengthening forth from a place beyond the new turn. Not understanding why, the sight brought on another bout of unwelcome nostalgia.

*Taliana had loved the heat; in the winter she'd hug herself to the pipe works in her chambers and in the summers she'd stand next to a fully loaded brazier and turn her face to the sun. She'd been like those stunted tomato plants, struggling to thrive but spirit willing to survive just the same. Poor woman. She'd never loved Ivanor, and yet she'd stayed - Solancei suspected, because of her. Dear Taliana...*

A crooked moment of lingering sadness settled over her, something that always pervaded whenever she thought that far back and it took a further edge off her fears. *Poor Taliana. It had been so long now and yet she remembered silly things*. Things like: as a child she'd never understood how they could heat the water all year round, nor how the furnaces would never seem to burn out although they had no trees for fuel. Then, when she'd turned four autumns old, her mother's maid had told her a story to inspire awe - *and ultimately enough curiosity* - to persuade her younger counterpart to go exploring to witness for herself.

Momentarily distracted in the past, Solancei was able to further repress the feeling of wrongness that prevailed in favour of the image of Taliana's face whilst she'd told her young charge the incredible fable of the never-dying flames directly beneath Ivanov's heart.

*For a wonder, the first Duke of Ivanor had fought and killed a dragon in the very place where they'd laid the castle foundations* - Solancei's lips twitched as they always did with thoughts of this particular memory – *and from there the fire spilt from the belly of that very beast, now served to keep everyone warm. 'That, and then of course a team of forty-one human minders and the green oil from under the ice', Taliana had told Solancei with a wink.*

Solancei still loved how Taliana had related the story with such persuasion, though. Still… she had wanted there to be a dragon on the bottom, rather than iron and oil; to her, there had somehow appeared to be a missing link.

*'But make no mistake child, Dragon Fire is forever-'*, the maid would tell Solancei, one plumb finger lifted in warning, *'-and you must beware for it will burn you to the heart… and deeper! So much deeper. Yes, beware!'*

And there was a memory that sent the smile fading.

The older woman had told her Dragons were but a myth in one blink, only to contradict with the strange statement about Dragon Fire the next, and Solancei was quite unexpectedly rushed by haunting regrets.

*Dear, dear Taliana.* Even had Solancei's younger self been there to watch the cremation, the remains of her mother's lady would've been gone in a flash: the fires whether dragon- or man-made, had burned with a heat that would emulate.

Quite unexpectedly, Solancei blinked. *And yet it would have mattered not. I would've been there, had I been given the chance. I swear I would!*

She swiped the edge of one vambrace across her forehead, absent-mindedly blinking again, as for a beat the memories of Ivanor soared, then crashed. *People died; memories were nice - but also useless! People died.* She wondered if Taliana had been scared. *It hardly mattered. People died...*

Solancei kicked back her head, raising her chin as though ready for a 'session' with Eso. There was a strange stench in the air that made her stomach churn. She had to stay away from the past; focus on the now! The mosaics were glistening like lizard scales: as though wet or slimy, when really they would be dry and hard; by now the stairs were so shallow that they were barely more than indents in the floor, and for a moment her head seemed to swim.

She felt odd, sneaking first a quick glance around the acute corner.

Then she straightened from a small crouch, bedazzled to realise she'd reached the top - *and that this was anything but!*

Lacking words, eyebrows climbing high, she exhaled pent-up breath and took a hesitant step forward, then another. *This... this she had not expected. Mercy... what was this?* The tunnel had ended just a handful of paces from the last direct corner; now before her, a roughly oval opening in the dark rock revealed an entrance through which the vast expanse of a cavern-sized space opened up beyond her present ability to comprehend.

Managing two more steps, she came to a slow grinding halt, dumbstruck by the temperature and sight. Expansive heat blanketed her, melting her ability to think. It was not the type of heat that would come from the sudden rays of sunshine on your face upon exiting from a dark stables into daylight, but rather a stripping, intense heat – dry, yet humid, as if twisted with a hint of steam. It felt unclean in her mouth, abrasive in her throat, somehow too heavy as her chest expanded, yet seemed to leave her dizzy with a lingering breathless sensation that left her unfulfilled.

Solancei gasped down another inhale, trying not to rush the thin air, though the temptation was there to hyperventilate. *Where the fleck had her feet and poor judgement taken her?*

Breathing through the sulphuric stench and her own incredulity, she moved forward, invariably hesitant as she glided deeper, now reaching the centre of a ledge that shared a certain likeness with the notion of a naturally-formed balcony within this colossal theatre. *Where the fleck indeed?*

Rumbled by unease, she stared around the semi-darkened cavity in mute sobriety - old misgivings soon sawing into her, thanks to the scene that spread before her: most of the walls without traceable limits, lost along with the idea of a ceiling to an undulating eerie darkness above and a fiery lit-up chasm below. *It was... it was certainly not like anything she remembered from Ivanor; in fact, it was a little beyond... everything.*

Swiping fingers across her damp brow, her guarded gaze floated to the place not far ahead, where the floor seemed to drop away into the rift. *She ignored the usual 'call'.* A sullen golden-red light, far richer in scale than any furnace flames she'd ever gazed upon, billowed from below as though out of an entrance that would lead her directly into Ulvaro'Cha's burrow...

*That inspired new memories. These not as pleasant as Ivanor.*

She shivered, assaulted by tendrils of her former unease. Super-heated air made gentle streamers of steam rise high to distort sight and pollute breaths with a pervasive stench that seemed alive and caustic. *Naturally, the ghosts of superstitions old, but deep, followed.*

Struck by futility, she mutely cursed the dread that was vying to overrule, then conquer, good sense. Yet, she could almost imagine the goddess' hot breath on her cheek, just as she could damned as near feel the deity, ugly with burns and ribbons of fire, rise forth in joyful anger to pull this fallen worshipper down into her pit!

*But why would the Goddess of Fear and Courage have permitted herself a simple pit deep within the ground?* If pausing for a blink to consider, it made no sense. Indeed, the Hag, 'The Taker of Tongues', would never have accepted this a suitable place of worship. She required subjects. *Lots of them; lines and lines of nervous, awestruck fools that could be seen to worship, and in turn see others do the same! This cave was dark, stinky, and clearly not at all frequented by anyone – possible-worshippers or not – so never in a hundred centuries would the Hag settle for this obscurity; never!*

She grimaced. Sure, Solancei might not appreciate the Gods but let it never be said that she did not know the Scripture or hadn't played to the foul creatures' tricks and whims regardless. She knew their ways. Mercy, had she not knelt in the dust before the idol of Anchan'Chi speaking the words of recognition with the King and Queen and Iambre; had she not helped arrange ten thousand roses in Silicia'Cha's temple in honour of the Goddess beauty and bounty; had she not cut her hair as an offering to sit atop the altar of Jethar'Chi the Lustful, so to keep Him from interfering in her life…?!

Well, she'd done that and more, and though she swallowed a sliver of dread now, she still knew herself right. This cavern – though grand – was neither golden nor accessible, and hence most definitely not the territory of a semi-sadistic goddess who loved to pitch worshippers against her petty whims and tricky pitfalls!

She sucked down a heavy breath, calming frayed nerves, hoping to bolster her softening stamina, and all of a sudden the heat seemed to rile; to mock.

*Ulvaro'Cha is a bitch that most recently cost me two pairs of new silk slippers and a favourite skirt,* it flashed through her mind with little chagrin that her respect for the deity would be found wanting. *With every visit I've had to donate every scrap of clothing left to me; I've had to leave her domain in an assembly of filthy, stinking rags not fit for swine, whilst Her priests snigger from up high, fanning themselves with lacy papyrus as they wear silks and gold!*

They called it a show of humility, of course – but it barely allowed a person a measure of decency, so no! Ulvaro'Cha would never stare anyone in the eye from the bottom of a pit under a giant fold of rock. *Never!*

Defiance rising, Solancei gazed around with more confidence than before, feeling the need to make this all okay - but for spite, this place appeared to offer no exit either, and she quivered with the onset of disappointment. *The flecking Gods be hanged! What would she have to do? What?*

Lashed by uncertainty, she closed her eyes for a beat to organise her thoughts. The image of the environment seemed to burn in her mind's eye, however, making it a difficult task. *Bloody rats, and that dip...!*

Opening her eyes as if compelled, she drifted towards the edge, the 'call' just not worth ignoring after all. *Something drew her, but it was ever so.* Usually she had to climb to get there – and in a way she supposed she had done today also, only not in the conventional sense. Mercy, but there was always 'something' indescribable about standing on the edge of the world, looking down... *something strangely grand that seemed fuelled by equal parts fey curiosity and morbid dread - sure, of course she did not understand the depths of it, but the 'call' of heights did not scare her. In fact, instead there'd always been an allure attached to doing the impossible; to reaching for the unobtainable, to look out on it all from the very top...*

The heat as she stepped forward though, was more stripping than she could've imagined even with her memories of Ivanor, and a strange feeling overtook her without warning, surprising her. *The temperature might scorch her face if she came any closer, and oddly, it gave her pause. Because oddly, this was one edge that did not seem to fascinate her after all. In fact, it did quite the opposite!*

Stretching awkwardly, she attempted to reach forward with her gaze instead, but the vertical drop was too steep and she could not see the bottom. The light, however - that angry and sullen gleam that did not seem to alter much, though it also never stayed quite the same from one blink to the next...

*That light was a most-temperate match to the searing heat that gushed forth like a silent explosion of fiery power, and something about it...*

As ever, she wanted to take that final step; she wanted to hover on the edge and look down, but she couldn't. *Her gut feeling would not allow it; her gut feeling – and something else...*

Backing up with a crease between her brows for the edgy sensations still playing concertina with her insides, she glanced around the platform, pondering what to do. The ledge shaped into a rough half-moon, the solid floor as flat as a Kheltian pancake, though with a distinctly downward tilt to the left that soon made you weary for the trick played on your senses. On either side, the natural podium ended in jagged walls and half-cast darkness, framed by an abundant spill of boulders and scree: the detritus left-over perhaps, either of a rock slide or maybe even from the tremor that had originally split the cavern in half.

*It was an imposing sight; it was certainly a spectacle to gape at; and it was, most assuredly, a definitive dead end!*

Weary of the heat and fire light that seemed to emanate and rise on thick vapours above the rim of the chasm, Solancei longed for daylight and easier times, and just like a curse, Taliana's jest about the dead dragon in the bowels of Ivanor flashed back into mind.

Slaying her bout of self-directed sarcasm for her own flaky imagination, she trailed to the nearest wall with a gripping sense of fatigue marching on her heels. *Now what?* In the stories no one ever seemed to know from whence the dragons came. *Perhaps they all lived in rivers of underground magma but were able to crawl out whenever the earth cracked open?*

She managed a half-smile for the whimsical thought – *fleck, or maybe sometimes lava was just lava, and stories just stories, and no one knew the details because whoever made them up had not bothered to include them!*

Feeling trapped, she rolled her eyes over her surroundings to pin the far ledge with a dull stare. It was just about visible but with the severed bedrock between her and it, the other side might as well have been leagues away - and if there was a way out, she'd never know from observing the crippled rock formations from afar.

An exasperated sigh escaped her. *She'd come so far; avoided Simaro and his soldiers… and for what? She'd have to go back.*

With a spike of frivolous anger towards the Gods, she bleakly wondered if *They* ever tired of laughing at her?

*So what the fleck did it matter whether she'd beg Them for favours or not? Whenever she'd most needed a little help, They'd never answered and she much suspected They would not move to raise a finger in aid now either. There was no bridge, rope or ladder, no nothing to help her cross the pit – and was this perhaps why no one had given chase? Because there was no other way out than the one Simaro had been going?*

It made her want to laugh with cynicism, but she could not make a sound. The feeling that this had all been for nothing was too queer; too final to accept, but then what?

Solancei looked at her hands and rubbed the palms against the thighs of her leathers feeling the semi-hardened hide soak up the sweat as though starved for moisture, then wiped a hand across her eyes, aware how the fatigue managed to lift an edge of her mental shield to worm under her hold on Veranto.

*She had to go back.*

She could look till she made herself blue in the face - all she'd achieve was a slightly nauseated feeling of dizziness, which arose when she tried to gaze past the distorted shadows as they shifted, spun and undulated to create forms in her imagination.

For a moment she simply watched as the vapours swirled like the gossamer veils of invisible dancers, in and out of focus, like madness come alive, so that for a blink she could almost imagine shapes moving within.

*And now I am seeing things that aren't there,* she taunted herself, blinking rapidly so that the half-formed images dissolved.

*She was spent.* What joy was there in knowing that whilst she might have succeeded in giving Simaro the slip, she would be stuck down here unless she crawled back? *Would she even be able to make it?*

She looked up, around the walls, smarting with desperation. *If there was foothold... a few handholds... some suitable outcrops that might be used... if she could climb... it'd been a while but-*

Her gaze fell back to the edge, trying to kindle the necessary mental attitude to follow through. *She could climb the boulders easily... well, all considering... the walls looked rugged enough for her to find a path and though it was unknown territory, then it might be done, but...*

But she'd never had to attempt such a feat under such duress before, nor in semi-darkness; already did she see that it was too risky and quelled a curse. *She might be desperate but she was not that stupid, and she had to face it: her former days of carefree personal disregard, married up with the questionable attitude of 'what-the-fleck-why-not', were in fact long gone. If she went to try this, Iambre would not approve...*

Weirdly, the sense of responsibility did not even sting and Solancei shook her head at the wall, feeling no pride in her achieved personal development, nor in the admission that she was no longer 'irresponsible'. *Contrary to what some believed, she'd never harboured 'a death wish', but there were perhaps a time where she might have thrown caution to the flames...*

She grimaced and massaged her brows between thumb and forefinger as she wasted another moment eyeing the edge with discomfort. *The invisible insects were back; she ignored them.* She had to turn herself around and walk back... *easy...* if only her mind had been able to command her body... *the insects were going mad, running faster and faster...*

Solancei acknowledged the 'something' wrong, round about the same time her skin started crawling in earnest; in her heightened state, she imagined seeing something from the corner of her eye, but...

She shrugged a shoulder, absently swiping the new perspiration off her forehead as she considered the far ledge, hoping that the State of Veranto would cancel out the sensations on her skin, but it didn't happen.

Instead, the Veranto tinkled too, raising the fine hairs on her body: enhancing the notion of 'something wrong'; enhancing the feeling of spiders without, a sense of fermenting unrest within. She couldn't have said how or why, but something seemed to draw her and as though taught caution by a master thief, her attention shifted in a blink.

*Again, she imagined seeing movement across the chasm, and maybe-?*

Narrowing her eyes, she stilled herself. *Was there something...? Something solidifying out of the darkness between the boulders opposite, or...?*

Prickly agitation turning to pins in her veins, she ran her eyes rapidly to the spot she'd marked out but vapours rising from the pit mocked the effort. There was nothing there...

*Guess I am just tired* - the self-recrimination was back - *more tired than after pulling an all-nighter training with Klaas and now my mind is finally bending!* Hunger... thirst... exhaustion... the Veranto must be tapping her reserves faster than she'd believed possible. *Why wouldn't her imagination be rife?*

She pulled back, not entirely comfortable with the effort required to push her body even that one small step. Behind her, the gentle slope of the stairwell wound its way back down toward the chilled bowels she'd come from, utterly unappealing – yet but for a blink, she felt an inexplicable and suddenly overwhelming urge to turn and run; it was like earlier; over her shoulder the mosaics glittered invitingly - like the rising sun catching the faceted crystals exposed on the walls of Oriana's Mountain back in Etruia. *There was no logic in this feeling; no real reason-*

A menacing growl descended out of thin air; the pitch unexpectedly sombre; the sound vibrantly coloured by an almost creeping, sentient menace... *tangible... physical... and something half-remembered...*

Mental pleasantries of Etruian landmarks shattering like fragile Tuxaman pastel-tinted crystal accidentally knocked from a precarious display, Solancei whipped her head toward the perceived threat so fast tendons kinked in her neck. Barely audible, the remnant sound oozed past skin and flesh to touch bones and spirit with a velvety caress of purring vibration, spreading a promise of winter; a drain on her reserves; a numbing of her mind; then-

*The terror struck her like a sucker-punch from an unsuspected foe.* Like a staining drop of oil it seemed something that had almost passed her by when it turned on her, offering pretence, if only for a split heartbeat, that containment and defence was somehow possible, but then-

Her lungs emptied on a soft exhale as primordial instinct extracted the marrow from her bones – *or maybe it was the bones melting from her marrow!* It made her knees wobble with new weakness and on the back of being robbed of strength, her guts seemed to contract, then liquefy as fear struck, sucking a greater hollow within.

Muscles cramping, in moments her senses immobilised as another growl echoed to surround and permeate: lingering impossibly long like an undertone of something forgotten.

*It made her want to lie down and beg for her life; it made her lighter than a snowflake with the urge to simply flee - but she could do neither. It was just like one other time: in a nightmare far, far away...*

Breath hitching again, she hiccupped for air. A rational part of her mind held on to a half-formed notion of 'canine' in the sound - still no dog had ever sounded like this: the clarity was foreign, the cadence tempered: too low and dangerous... *a warning... a promise...* a herald of 'Ending' - and for one confusing, misconstrued blink, the idea returned that she knew this sound; that she had heard something similar before, but that was simply… *impossible.*

Because she couldn't help the need, she walked her eyes back towards the chasm - the flash goosebumps flooding from shoulders down her arms and back, carrying no reference to the physical, as the Veranto link diminished in a blink, retracting as though of tangible sentience.

The fright of losing it, snapped her to attention - a cutting blade of ice, simultaneously severing fear and lending space for the return of sense beyond mindless instinct.

*Mercy, what was happening? Where had she heard this before?* As unexpected as the first growl, a queer memory tugged. *One hag-ridden dream blossoming; the lurching pull of a carriage about to plummet into nothing; the sound of nightmares shadowing! But no… that wasn't real! That had never been real, at least-*

*At least not to her!*

Across the chasm, the shadows shifted… and solidified.

# A New Tutor

"Ankh'Sheriti-Nefer'Kemnebit, my lotus! My heart smiles to see you, Beloved Daughter!"

The pleasant greeting brought the girl back to the present, instantly, as though someone had snapped their fingers in her ear, but as her head flew up she nevertheless knew a heartbeat of surprise, to find herself still under the royal awning, and not upon a field in some unknown lands, far off.

"As does mine heart to feel your presence, dear Sire." Nefer managed, almost by default as He-Who-Is' slanted eyes held her gaze with curious interest, the silver star pupils so like her own, shining softly with His inner power. Enhanced by powdered gold-leaf and azure to complement the hues of his pleated belt and knee-long kilt of identical colours, He appeared a welcome familiar distraction; one that she might cling onto without regret, for with His recognition of her and by the calling of her Name, the last vestiges of her vision crumbled before the power of His presence.

Seemingly pleased with her response, her father gave her a casual wave and motioned for her to rise. The heat billowed and for a moment, all Ankh'Sheriti-Nefer'Kemnebit could see, was the willowy-strong form of the Mshai as he rippled before her eyes, the pain of the injury suffered earlier finally forcing him to his knees in defeat: two worlds overlapping...

*This was not right but somehow she managed to stay collected, though she still longed to learn why the Mshai had betrayed them.*

"So Dear Heart, what brings you out here today?" her Sire enquired with just enough interest to appear genuinely intrigued. "Did you perchance sense that I was going to call for you?"

Lost for words, she hesitated. *Call for her?* She knew she must answer but her mind was still on the vision.

Mistaking her quiet for shyness, the two men exchanged quick looks of indulgent understanding. It didn't go unnoticed by her and she felt a little tingle of annoyance: she had seen that kind of look before and she was not *that* young anymore; she did not just interrupt His meetings like a spoilt child whenever she wanted – she was following protocol and this was important! *Her tidings warranted the Council's due consideration and adult respect! The sooner He sent her on her away, the better.*

Silently she regained her feet. She felt time wasted trickle by with every heartbeat. *Wasting... wasting...*

A small child would possibly stamp her feet and make demands in the hope that an indulgent father would let her run along, but not her now. To be taken seriously, one must act accordingly, and so she mustered patience, crossed both arms before her chest and bowed from the waist. *Gracefully. Like a lady.*

Eyes down she shouldered the appropriate five heartbeats with a patience she did not feel thus allowing Him to know her heartfelt respect. "He-Who-Is-Our-Land-and-Future, merciful Sire, I ask of you to hear me, for I have a vision for the Queen and request her location."

Keeping the information to a minimum before the unknown visitor, Nefer'Kemnebit put just a little urgency into her tone, allowing her Sire to discern her need for haste. Her vision was for the ears of the Council only until deemed otherwise by the Chief of Vectors, or indeed by He-Who-Is Himself, and since her Sire was busy...

Watching her father cast the sliver of a mirthful smile in the visitor's direction, Nefer'Kemnebit calmly awaited his answer, though she felt like shouting for them to stop this imbecile behaviour. What she needed, was her Mama - and even more importantly, the ears and minds of the Council - not a show of affection from her Sire, however much she might otherwise normally enjoy it.

As though reading her thoughts, He-Who-Is ventured, "Beloved Daughter, I am sad that you seek only the company of your Esteemed Mother - and thereby I take it - the stuffy presence of our Historian Council, but how could it surprise me?"

With a smile for his visitor who'd been watching her with polished patience and a true sparkle of interest within his deep-set, blue eyes, her Sire continued, "Best-Loved Daughter, I sense your need for haste, yet nevertheless it would please me greatly if you could stay just a small measure of time to share the refreshment with me and my esteemed visitor before seeking out our dearest Tanafriti Nafretiri. We have just concluded our discussions and were about to enjoy some sugared loaf and iced fruits – please Lotus-of-my-Heart, join us for a while? The Best-Loved Queen is resting and will not see herself disturbed until the golden eye is past noon and besides, I have some news..."

"Resting?" For a blink, Nefer's mind zoned-in only on the thing that mattered to her. *Was her mother resting? Again?*

Her heart sank with the thought but then, despite everything, Nefer'Kemnebit felt a sudden small sliver of excitement to be invited by her Sire to join Him and his guest. It was nothing short of what He would have asked an honoured adult and she felt a flush of affection that He would want to keep her in His presence until her Mama emerged from the apartments. At the same time though, she felt almost quite unable to sit down as well when she carried such important information and Nefer felt herself waver before she thought the better of it.

She could decline of course, but it would be very impolite and she might disappoint her Sire for the 'offence' – a thing she did not relish the thought of doing. The golden eye was riding much higher already and her Mama would not be long. The iced fruits did look so very juicy and they were already beginning to melt in their alabaster bowls. *Could she truly find any harm in pleasing her father?* Certainly, if she paused to think about it, then surely she could find no harm as great as disturbing her Mama if she'd retired. The First Queen was with child again but this pregnancy had been trying for her mother – or so she'd been led to believe, for she'd had no visions to substantiate the statements. There could, however, be no denying that Nafretiri's belly was now so distended that even Nefer'Kemnebit understood why her Mama would want to lie down. Carrying an extra load like that looked very uncomfortable indeed - and that her Mama had needed to leave her in favour of some rest could come as no surprise at this stage, although then the notion of a test…?

Nefer'Kemnebit shifted her mind from the thought. She had seen enough pregnant women around the complex to know that her Mama – *the Proud Nafretiri* - was not so particularly different from any of the other when it came to matters like that.

It was 'inconvenient', but making the best of the situation Nefer nodded once then and came closer at her father's behest. She would not presume to occupy the third seat without invite, but she needn't wait on her feet for long as the servants hovering just beyond view jumped to fetch her another without the need of verbal instructions. Well-trained, they carried out their role effortlessly and before she could straighten from planting two affectionate kisses on her Sire's dark cheeks, a wide chair - made comfortable by numerous brightly covered cushions - stood ready to receive her.

Gesturing for her and His visitor to help themselves to food and drinks, He-Who-Is' dark eyes remained on her face. Unreadable. And yet she offered him a smile. With the lack of serving maids or cup-bearers, Nefer's earlier deductions seemed both sustained and flawed. If her Sire valued His visitor, offering equal status, there should've been a river of servants in attendance, but the fact that there was not, made her speculate. *She'd been drilled in customs and decorum; she knew when proceedings deviated from the norm, and this wholeheartedly did. Why was this stranger different?* Her Sire had made no attempt to introduce her - indeed He did not have to of course, but as her curiosity grew she hoped He would. Rarely had she seen her Sire flounder time on one-man audiences like this, nor had He usually the time to stay during the enjoyment of refreshments. *Was this a social meeting of two friends or a private business appointment?*

Whatever the occasion, however, she did not let it stop her now that she had been made welcome and she tucked into the iced mangoes with much enjoyment of the simple pleasure their cool, juicy flesh brought her.

Without realising it until she tasted the ripe pieces of fruit, she was ravenous. Her visions often left her famished - only for all of her hunger, she still knew better than to gorge herself in front of a stranger; thus far she'd behaved suitably mature and she'd better carry on.

Watching her for short moments, the two adults followed her lead though in a slightly more restraint manner, loading only a fraction of each dish onto their small golden plates. Silence ruled, allowing Nefer'Kemnebit a chance to tuck into her fifth piece of fruit without rush.

Then the stranger spoke, "So, I see that Queen Nafretiri's beauty is already budding in this lovely daughter of yours, Esteemed One."

Looking pleased with the comment, He-Who-Is nodded in agreement, offering Nefer'Kemnebit a smug look that held much affection. She returned the sentiment and her father's ebony face split in an assuring smile: a quick flash of white, even teeth – *so like her own: not quite Human, not quite Heirah-Noor Elvern; not quite Sabén-Heshep...*

Belatedly she realised that she should've acknowledged the stranger's kind compliment too and quickly bent her head in thanks, but the older man seemed unconcerned with the glitch in manners, as he looked her over.

"I see your eyes and her mother's graceful neck. Truly, I have been made aware that she is already a valuable asset to the Esteemed One's family, but with matters the way they are, I suspect that she will ever be far too valuable to wed off to even the most worthy of suitors?"

The stranger's comment was barely a question as much as a statement of fact and yet, raising a questioning eyebrow in her father's direction, the older visitor boldly added, "I have a great-grandson of a relative, of course, should you ever wish to solidify our lines but I too can see that grooming her for something much more beneficial than a stuffy old marriage, will suit her very well."

Between bites, Nefer'Kemnebit paid close attention. She wasn't sure if she liked all this talk of marriage and beauty right in front of her. That was the stuff for true adults, not girls, and she had no wish to wed now - or later for that matter. She partly suspected that her standing would require her to do nothing less though since Mama often hinted at the possibility, but it was nothing she wished to worry about, for the Queen also hinted at many other things.

Watching the older man to gauge his intentions, she partly forgot about her delicious meal as his dark-blue eyes suddenly returned her gaze. They were kind eyes, she thought then - *the Human aspect was interesting* – and yet they seemed to be eyes that had seen much and endured, and for a moment she wondered at his age. There was something oddly age-less about the old man's unblemished hands, about his smooth yet crinkled forehead and about his proud, straight-backed bearing, which all struck a chord in her. Even though she was well-used to seeing the common traits of ageless grace amongst her Father's people, this visitor was somehow different. For one, she suspected the white hair meant that he would have seen the passing of centuries, maybe even a millennium or more - and though it was no lie that Time was easy on her people, even such an impressive life-span had been known to bend an Elvern back with age; with the sum of experiences. And yet...

*And yet, it didn't matter.* There were many a strange exceptions to the rule in the Realm of Sabén-Heshep; her father was a good judge of character and He appeared to like the man. That was all she need know and was she perchance already wise enough to understand that not everything was as it seemed, she secretly decided to reserve her judgement, just as Mama had often cautioned her - a good thing perhaps, for the stranger's next words fell even more indecently forward than earlier.

"So Ankh'Sheriti-Nefer'Kemnebit, He-Who-Is, tells me that you have inherited more than the colour of those lovely eyes from your late grandmamma: I see that you have also the gift to read the spelled shards of the route to the futures! That is a powerful Affinity at that for one so young, but tell me Sheriti: how goes your exercises? Can you command your gift at ease or do the visions direct you?"

The older man smiled at her. *A kindly smile,* she thought, *full of Human teeth.* Nefer'Kemnebit felt herself stare and looked from the stranger's broad features to her Father's angular and back again before remembering herself and her manners. *How would this man know the difference and why had her father given this stranger such knowledge about her? He was not a fellow Seer; she'd never sensed him or seen him or communicated with him – not physically, and certainly not through her Sight either.*

Uncertainty washed over her and her eyes strayed a little towards He-Who-Is. Watching her father's encouraging nod from the corner of her eye, however, she obeyed His silent consent, but reluctantly, feeling more than a little unnerved to share such personal details with a total stranger.

"Hetshepsu-" she began, addressing the odd, white-haired man with the honorific title in lieu of his unknown name, "-I see that you have my Sire's ear and heart, so forgive my ignorance, I am but unaccustomed to sharing knowledge of my gift with strangers. This will not happen again – forgive me."

The stranger smiled in a small, but genuine way, at her choice of words. *The line of those Human teeth was amazing,* she thought, *all straight and square and in that respect quite Elvern - but with barely a point to the two single canines he did have, and completely missing the second, larger and usually sharper set of these that marked all her people as the once-predators they'd been at the dawn of creation before the Maker gave them temperance and reasoning.*

"Sheriti, Dearest Daughter of the Esteemed One,-" Nefer startled as the man began to speak but offered her attention happily enough, as he continued, "-you honour me with a title far beyond my standing and were I ever such a high-ranking man, you would have no need to address me so formally, anyhow. You see, I have been in service of this realm for longer than memory recorded in song and on vellum, and there are some things I would not presume to change, including my standing with the Esteemed Watchéran's house. Now the truth of the matter is that He–who-is has gracefully allowed me to visit your wondrous lands in exchange for a small favour this time, and Sheriti dear, would it stress you overly much to learn that I have agreed to oversee the continued development of your gift for the foreseeable future?"

Nefer'Kemnebit nearly choked. Forgetting to remain a lady, she stopped her careful chewing mid-bite and simply stared. Around the fruit in her mouth she somehow managed an unsteady, "But why?"

The visitor smiled, "My dear girl that should be obvious. Now that Queen Nafretiri is about to grant our Living God yet another present of life, she will doubtlessly be otherwise occupied and so it's only proper that someone else looks after your education full-time, don't you agree?"

Speechless, Nefer'Kemnebit watched the man say the words as though it was straightforward when in fact, it was not so at all. *Well… not for her anyway! To her, this was completely unexpected!*

Swallowing the bite of suddenly tasteless fruity pulp, she regarded her Sire's proud expression. *He'd been about to call for her. This was why.* The visitor was not throwing empty words - that much was certain or her father would not have sat there quietly - but that she would someday have to trust in a stranger and not her Mama, had simply never occurred to her. Nafretiri had been pregnant times before but had always been there to guide and help her despite the new child in her life. *Why was it different this time?* Confusion took her aback.

Seeing the worry in her pale eyes, the old stranger smiled reassuringly as he made a disarming gesture. "My dearest, where are my manners now? In my overwhelming joy to make your acquaintance, dear heart, I forget myself. Oh, but how could I be so rude? I fear my dishonour is complete! Please, if the Watchéran might be good enough to introduce me, then perhaps…?"

Her Sire smiled, "If you so wish it, Speaker."

The other man nodded, "Yes. Yes, I should think it only right considering…"

"Nefer, my dear heart," her Sire turned His gaze to hers, "allow me to introduce our esteemed guest then. This is Mshai Sinuhé Sedjem-Alhath'naar, Suten Hamu and Urshé to the Sabén-Heshep."

Crossing his arms solemnly over the narrow chest - finally displaying a little more than a hint of the foreign benedictions painted upon his wrists - the man Sinuhé, bowed respectfully from the waist, showing Nefer'Kemnebit equal rights to that of an adult. His eyes were still kind, but even so, she'd have returned the honour without thinking. The coincidence of learning that this man was of a similar primary profession as the blue-haired Mshai of her visions, was almost too much and a small chill travelled down her back despite the hot weather. It reminded her acutely that she had important matters to see to, only now she didn't know what to do about it and she remained silent as her new mentor straightened, lowering his arms.

As though the Watchéran was aware of her reluctance to recognise this new addition to their household, her father broke into her thoughts, "My Beautiful Lotus, be kind and treat this man well. Indeed, though he is modest, he used to answer to the very title of 'Hetshepsu', which you so aptly awarded him without knowing of his past. For the Maker, he chose to give up this title and much more besides – and in his pursuit of knowledge to guide us all in the pursuit of a secure future, we owe him and his brethren much. Understand that the very fact the Mshai Sinuhé has agreed to aid us - *to aid you* - is indeed an honour beyond compare."

Hesitating just a blink beyond polite, Nefer nodded meekly, but she still could not hide the lingering disquiet from her father, who saw and added, "My Dear Heart, this man has more understanding of your gift and of what to do with it, than any of the existing council members put together and Mshai Sinuhé is loyal. He is the only worthy teacher to replace your Mama. You must trust in him and listen. That is all I have to say."

Nefer lowered her eyes. Quicker to respond this time she said, "Yes of course Esteemed One."

# How the Cult Hunts

Tasting the metallic tang of fear she hadn't known in years, Solancei was abruptly taken back to her childhood: to the dreams that had haunted her for too long until the Chief had managed to teach her how to dispel their power. Almost she pinched her own arm. *Was she hallucinating? Sleepwalking?*

Another growl laced itself into her, playing trivia with her need to live, and she felt the State of Veranto waver then, like one of her gossamer veils ripped loose during a canter. In counter, she slapped a hard-won hair's-worth of will into maintaining the Link, feeding it what spark she could, though turmoil boiled. *It was most assuredly too little, but...*

An involuntary spasm rode through her and it was fraught with queer sensations. Then a lilting rattle of shifting metal played forth: a barely audible tune; the subtle tinkle of segments running over stone... *soft, slithering, eerie...*

An apparition followed. Through the haze, something showed in the shadows of the opposite ledge - something out of nowhere... humanoid, but not. *Crouching, then standing, then roaming forth, then disappearing: amidst the dark fissures and cathedral tons of rock, the figure was there, then not, then-*

She wiped strain and sweat from her eyes. The unnamed terror rolled within her, ceaseless, nudging and reshaping the Veranto, but the air seemed thick with trickery, erasing true vision as she blinked.

Then a new expanding growl speared her… *old death riding on the bones of chaos: as inevitable as her next breath, so it would claim her.*

It left her dazed, as for a heartbeat she both crumbled and died, yet ran and lived, and in the infinite space in between she sampled submission. Her vision flickered, darkening, then brightening. *Something was there… not there… there…*

Touching her shoulder with a red-scaled hand of dark claws and long spindly fingers, something too fey beyond the confinement of nightmares seemed to breathe in her ear, bringing images…

She shook herself, an involuntary sound of revulsion escaping her like a guttural bark. *Something old wrapped its will around hers just the same; something too elusive to see; something too substantial to ignore.*

Solancei's heart lurched and she might have cried out again as shadow red-and-black touched her mind, then she was alone on the lip of rock, but on the ledge opposite, the figure she'd thought 'imagined', continued to glitch into reality: like an illusion seen pushed into life during the flash-blinks of lightning.

Too frightened by the sight, she realised this might just be something feeding off her thrall-like emotions, yet she could not fight nor deflect. She swallowed, but her mouth was too dry again; the feeling too detached from reality somehow. She ripped her eyes away from the strange sight a hundred times, yet she never managed to move. Down to her marrow, she was quivering – the sensation intensifying, mad thoughts developing life. *Maybe she was hallucinating! Maybe she'd stayed linked to the State of Veranto for too long, too deeply, and was now beginning to suffer the effects, or... or...*

But there was a darkness pooling where she'd kept her eyes locked; a shade of pitch too heavy for shadow, solidifying... *solidifying...*

Again, she heard the subtle song of chain on stone, then silence, and-

Darker than midnight at new moon, a shadow-veiled figure stared back at her from the centre of the other ledge; something of insidious malice and vicious longing; something sensed, yet ever not quite seen, ripped and clad in the darkest cloth of Human fear: twisted life poured into shape, like inky treacle teased from the bottom of a deep jar.

With a succinct staccato edge to movement belying nature, the sinuous shapeshifted suddenly, shedding darkness – or maybe transforming it – to materialise further. Like she'd witnessed before, it moved with a sense of strange glitches that toyed with perception, mirroring madness - something impossible for the eye to follow, though the senses did not mistake a thing whilst the shadow became whole.

She blinked, then blinked again - but fluid solidity belonging to water, a creation of dark-red scales glided forward on its ledge, trailing a fine segmented chain attached to something at the neck – a tracing of pale metal flashing like jets of diamond despite the low cadence of light.

For a blink, triangular yellow-green eyes reflected fire in multiple facets as the apparition twisted slightly to behold her with

a heavy growl of greeting from the depths of its throat. It was a sound that suddenly seemed a lingering pulse overlaying her own - biting like the rasping of ancient voices in her mind - too alien to comprehend.

It made her sway on her feet. A deep hiss ended the challenge, repulsing even had she not seen the reflection of low light flicker across ebony sickle-like claws and rows of needle-point teeth packed into an obscenely wide maw, from which slipped a line of slaver.

As though to break a spell, the thing snapped its teeth with menacing detachment just once - a sharp, inhuman click to stir notions of splintering bones, and Solancei jumped back as though it had touched her, shivering wildly within her skin.

*She was rarely thrown by anything.* In fact, as Iambre's Shield she could not allow herself to pause over even the most irregular or unusual event, but right then she had no voice, no breath, no will.

She'd never encountered anything like this - not in stories, not in documents. The horror possessed two arms, two legs; it faced her upright like a man, hunched as though from hard labour - but all the proportions were wrong: the joints crooked, the limbs too long, the teeth-

*The teeth certainly not Human!*

She licked her lips nervously. From what she could see, red-black scales covered the creature's ascetic, emaciated body just like those of a snake - yet if the 'thing' seemed of a lithe composition, she was inspired to think it neither fragile nor weak, for it held itself with coiled, predatory vibe that warned of speed and strength. Together with the spikes seen along a ridged, trailing tail, she was inspired to think of a weapon made flesh, yet how could that be possible? How could any of this be real?

Consternation flooding forth, Solancei clenched her teeth against emotions suddenly twisting imaginary daggers in her bowels. *What was she looking at? How did that fit in with the world? If she was not mad; if her eyes were true, was this one of Arbar'Chi's feared messengers? Or a cursed Spirit? Or... or was it perchance even a Demonai?*

Suppressing old feelings experienced only in hag-ridden dreams, she raked-in a breath through her teeth, almost forgetting to exhale.

The apparition snarled – and angry quiver, revealing teeth. *Too many teeth...*

It stopping her dead as it *'glitched'* again, hunching slightly as it re-solidified yet a little further forward than before, shifting within the blink of an eye from visible to wispy smoke, to nothing, then back. *Unreal eyes of another world kept her bound to the spot, however. Clever, weighing eyes. Eyes that filled the space and ate everything; ate her courage.*

With the Veranto link swaying like a dancer but finally aiding her, Solancei drew back a halting step, only belatedly feeling the strain of this small movement when her leg muscles seemed to cramp, working against her wishes.

In turn, the creature hissed. She couldn't have explained how, but for a blink she sensed something else had hooked its attention. *It was not much, but then…*

Like a celebrated breeze on a hot day, the ooze of fear that tied her down lifted, dissolving the mist of her temporary madness. It was less than she needed for sanity, but still enough to gain new strength, and with a twine of gossamer finer than spider silk, hope tied itself to her, encouraging her to attempt another step of retreat.

*It was all she got.*

Like a taunting jester offering riddles of deceit, the fragile weave of relief pulled apart. It seemed a cruel trick. The reprieve had been too short. A whisper of despair saddled her just as another creature identical to the first horror, suddenly winked into life like a phantom of vapour and torment, for the second time draining her of personal choice.

A sound she wouldn't have recognised escaped her. *Things still-alive did not materialise nor glitch into sight! In stories, genies and wizards 'materialised', but not in real life!*

For a blink she lost sight of self and purpose, but the weight of the twin creatures' dead gazes belied her hysteric denial. With their very presence they assaulted the senses, forcing her acceptance of them; forcing her to believe them real, because the State of Veranto would not be enough: eventually, she'd find herself on her knees, something she'd never allow to happen if only hallucinating, and then…

She closed her eyes to escape their hungry, alien attention but it seemed futile. The identical symmetry of the horrors burned her mind. *One creature snarled, glitching. Then teeth snatched at her. Warring...*

Her eyes flew open. Staggering in fright of the sudden painful, inches long gash in her arm, she fell backwards, imagining those teeth slicing across her skin. *Imagining-*

She staggered back another step, evading... *but death was stalking her; eyes tearing up, she moved to clutch her arm, to staunch the blood-*

Struck by confusion, Solancei let her hand drop. Her shirt was intact and her skin unbroken. The two creatures were not near her; were still tethered behind the veils of warm air and streamers; bound on the opposite ledge.

Head reeling, body momentarily broken off its strange paralysis, she shuffled backwards like a drunkard not in control of her own body but determined to make headway regardless.

*It felt weird. She was fighting herself.* One of the creatures hissed, the sound of water on smouldering coal somehow obscenely normal; as though angered the other horror directed a swipe of sickle claws back at it, raising obvious discord, as the twin creature fell back with a snarl and a wide yaw of warning.

A sour smell bloomed. *She sensed hate like a perfume.* The other nightmare growled, turning at the offence like a rabid dog to snap in warning at its twin and Solancei cringed, feeling the click of teeth ride into her mind like a freak exhibition of discord and song.

As chains rattled, their hatred seemed to bleed into her mind as though she knew their hearts – it was like the aura coming off Iambre on a bad day, only deeper - those low growls that struck like physical vibration within her core, were sensations too hard to vanquish. For a blink, one of the snarling creatures seemed suddenly so close again that she could feel its dry, sweet breath whistling past the rows of needles near enough to take a bite out of her cheek, then the feeling vanished, leaving a strange stain in her mind - *a blob of something she did not want but could not dislodge.*

Solancei gripped the seax till the pressure seemed enough to mould an imprint of her fingers on the wooden handle. It was a bit of solidity in a world gone afloat into a realm of absurdity; an anchor, but-

*'We will hunt.'* She heard the promise on a growling vibration that went past the Veranto and might have stopped her dead for good but for the expanding ice in her veins that seemed to rise like a wall within - oddly numbing; viciously defensive. It was something she might have achieved through the State of Veranto, but she didn't recognise the particular 'strain' and that too played havoc with reality. *'Hunt... Come hunt!'*

Head spinning just once, another jab of fear probed her but this one felt animalistic - not hers, though it hit her like a breath of blue smoke.

*Demonai,* it flicked like lightning and char through her mind. *What else can they be? They must be Demonai: monsters that hide in the dark and eat dogs and babies! Demonai like those told of in nursery rhymes to frighten children into behaving or else! Mercy, and did the tales not tell of the creatures abilities' to cast images and make a person mad?*

Solancei clenched her teeth hard, experiencing a new measure of dark hysterics as her mind rebelled against the unreal deduction, yet suddenly she no longer thought that Demonai ate only babies or dogs!

The seax began to tremble, her fingers quivering as though under strain. *Is there comfort in knowing that you might be quite ready for a trip to the asylum after this? Or will there ever be comfort now?*

Again something seemed to brush against her thoughts, jolting her: a slightly odd, feather-light sensation, which was softy insistent as it touched her with a glimmer of something she could not decipher until the sudden unbidden image of a grazing horse rode into her mind's eye. *It was like a memory. It had the shape of a memory, but-*

Alarmed at the 'invasion', she tried to rip her eyes from the creatures but the picture in her mind expanded - sinking her deeper, removing her from the present. *And in a flash, she saw more monsters manifest. They were feasting: frenziedly tearing at the horse with teeth and abandon, and she perceived that they'd hunted the creature: used their cunning and skill to unite in a... - a 'Cult'? - ...but one horse presented little challenge, and the Cult - the pack – had barely sated their lust.*

Solancei pushed at the image instilled upon her, but it was not enough. For one infinitesimal blink, she'd felt the warmth of blood roll into her mouth as she looked through eyes not her own and ripped into a hunk of horse flesh with strength and pleasure likewise never hers to begin with.

*Within moments she was drunk with the pleasure of warm, raw meat and something... something strangely alluring, like... like a secret nectar flowing in her veins - and she wanted more! Magic, they whispered, give us magic! More! Always more!*

Disgusted, Solancei stumbled back from the illusion with a strangled cry, a freaky coldness spreading within her - for mercy finally breaking the Demonai's strange hold.

Her body already reacting, she bolted, but could not out-manoeuvre the series of events she'd borne witness to. *Mercy! It was just too visual. Too visceral. The ascetic horrors feasted on the horse like starved hyenas, the short spikes along their bony spines shivering with the ferocity of their onslaught as they devoured. It was horrendous, yet beautifully simple! Breathe, hunt, kill, eat...*

Solancei's mind grappled free of the image as she rounded the corner of the corridor banging her shoulder against the rock and not caring as it spun her wide. *The reptilian sooty-red hides of her fellow Cult were not quite ebony to the eye, but they came close... so close even, that the blood that ran like juices from gluttony, looked little more than rich oil upon their flat faces and smooth scales...*

With a sound of disgust, she flung herself forward with more speed in outright effort to force out the images – *the memories* – as she stumbled and ran.

Lying helped. To a point.

*It was not real! It could not be real! Demonai were imaginary beasts invented to scare children into staying in bed!*

Like a prayer, Solancei repeated those words over and over, pushing her hands over her face in time with the new-found mantra as if that might clear the pictures in her mind's eye, but she knew the creatures had done something to her and the pleasure of slaughter haunted her down the corridor. *That... and the grinning, green-eyed Demonai as it purred at her...*

Barely seeing where her feet fell, she continued the mad flight, choking on something that could never rightly be digested. *It was over so fast – the horse would've never sensed the original threat of their presence - they were little more than shadows -* she understood that somehow, just as she understood that they are little more than that which moves in the corner of an eye in a breath between heartbeats.

*And at first attack, the 'meat' had bolted – which was good - and the thrill of its fear had become like an intoxicant to their senses then. This made them stronger; faster –* she understood this also, now - *the horse, however, did not. It might have kicked out, its squeals too high-pitched for their inner ear-spirals not to hurt - but it was already too late, and as their Retz Ken 'roamed' from the shadows then, claiming the 'Trophy', there'd already been another – the strongest of the remaining pack – rising to leadership as the Cult caught scent of new prey. This one... this one perhaps human!*

Empty stomach turning, Solancei retched, her run down the steps little more than a blindly, indelicate lurch. A many-headed monster of panic clawed deeper, and with it, exquisite repulsive understanding. *The creatures she'd locked eyes with in the cavern had been Retz Ken! They were both powerful and had slain many and claimed even more!* It was chaos. It was dread. It was impossible. Yet 'impossible' was not a word she'd ever use again; almost she could still taste the blood...

'*Bastard creature-*', she yelled in her thoughts, wits failing, ice pushing, '-*get out of my mind! Get out!*'

But the new Retz Ken would lead the 'Cult' onwards then. She could see it. And the Hunt was good! The Hunt was everything!

...'*And we will hunt!*' The words seemed to be thrown at her from afar with blood-curdling promise. '*We will hunt... and your light will be ours! The call has been made!*'

Solancei's stomach rolled again.

Icy, yet burning warm, she felt detached from her body's demands and sped up the pace. The images seemed to finally splinter under distance and demand then, yet as they did, she saw one final shadow lurch up in her mind's eye: something that seemed to hunger even worse than the two Demonai she'd run from, and it was telling her it was only ever a question of time!

# Yielding to the Present

Panic soaring, Solancei felt her mind do a sideways shift, something akin to an evasion. *It was only an illusion.* Of course, she knew this! But…

*'Get control'*, a lucid sensible part of her seemed to yell within her own head, *'Get control! What is happening to you is impossible! The Veranto is still strong! Use it!'*

But the impossible no longer existed. Those creatures had been in her head; in her mind! Maybe they still were…?

Poised to splinter into a hundred pieces, the anticipated ruin never came. Something feral flared icy and hot within her core, brutally severing that lingering feeling that those 'things' were still riding along in her head. It saved a spark - *mercy somehow it ignited a semblance of her usual mettle* – and she emerged on the safe side of panic, feeling utterly spent and barely in control of her faculties, but at least with the mental 'upper hand' once more back in her court.

Breathing hard, she slowed her manic run to a rapid walk. In the wake of madness, a wave of emotion rolled within her core and she swallowed sour bile. *Demonai were not real! How could they be?*

She tried to grin but the effort was weak, her bravado dead. She did not know what to think but it seemed that her thoughts were once more quiet, her feelings too, yet if her head was now blessedly silent, she could still remember. *The taste of blood had been too real… and she'd liked it!*

Drenched in sweat, yet cold to the core, she could not seem to shake off the primeval drive she'd felt. *Something about the flow of fear and control... the heat of new blood in her mouth... rather than diminish it seemed to be spreading like a malignant corruption of her spirit. Pervasive... demanding... incurable.*

With a small yelp of revulsion against the track of her own mind, Solancei abandoned hope of slashing it through denial. *She did not need to recover! She needed to run and never stop! If she could gain distance then maybe...*

Lungs burning like spilt acid, she flung herself forward, breaking into a hard run once more. The seax was still in her hand but the weapon seemed pointless. Her breath came fast and sparse; beneath her feet, the shallow steps seemed to fly by, but she could not bring herself to stop again.

*What would happen when she reached the darkness below?* She didn't care; the darkness seemed preferable now! *Gods, and those red scales - the same rich shade as blood from the vein polluted by soot!*

She pushed at the image, flushed by new horror as she ran. She could not recall ever being so off-kilter before. It was like she could not control her own feelings; as if the State of Veranto had never been a factor, and the pictures in her mind seemed to suck her right back in if she gave herself a moment to dwell! There was a coldness in her - so in-like any she'd ever experienced, even when standing on the edge of her parents gravesite all those long years ago - and for every pace, a bone-splitting spear of that cold seemed to race through her core, ciphering down every muscle and nerve-ending, firing up extra strength so that she might run faster. *Demonai or animals, to them you are prey! Run!*

Mind shivering, she shied away from the thoughts. Through the Veranto she tried to control it but the link seemed brittle and secondary, a thing which might vanish on an exhale or a cough. Without the link she'd be a crumbling wrack of pain on the floor: exhaustion and injuries would catch up – another frightening possibility she could not bear to think of either - and so she must gain distance; run…

Panting as though she'd already run miles, Solancei allowed her boots to find the steps of their own accord. There was a mad urge within her; a kind of knowledge even - something she could not define, although she felt it might probably end up defining her.

*Madness… could it be madness?* If she conquered her fear and went back, would there even be any creatures in that cavern? And would she even see the same? Feel the same? This was-

From somewhere impossibly far, yet rooted in a corner of reality, she imagined a slight jingle… *an idea of footfalls not her own…*

It was a thought that caught like an echo; a distraction: enough to carve a path past the images in her head. *Enough to-*

A stab of surprise, then alarm, flashed and died. For a blink, she could not tell the imagined from the real. She was light-headed; her defences too skewed for her to form a strategy. *The sounds of people were so mundane, twisted by the flow of the corridor, rendered impossible to judge.*

She looked at the swirling mosaics. *She didn't belong here. Her mind seemed sluggish; hazy...*

The men came into view as she was still trying to control her indecision, their appearance as unreal as a dream: Zanzier soldiers in yellow and blue looking out of place in their smart sashes and heraldry.

For a blink her mind swirled with colours; she could make no sense of numbers – there were not many, yet the tunnel was instantly blocked just the same - and she felt strangely blinded to action as that lingering coldness travelled down her core in a stripping rush of detachment. *A pause... an eternity...*

As an attest of confidence, the soldiers' short swords were sheathed but it did not make the men seem less alert as they suddenly stood face to face and her chill seemed to speak directly to her then, leaving her with a strangely disconnected concept that she must either kill them all or else lose every advantage she'd gained in slipping away from the cell in the first place.

She blinked, the action too slow for reality; out of sync.

*Kill them...?* Yes, she could do that - the flash of something icy and merciless seemed to sparkle within her at the prospect; it made the State of Veranto feel wrong, but-

*Kill them all... yes... and kill the Demonai... and be safe.*

The descending haze deepened. There was a loss of coherency between thought and will, but the ice in her core was solidifying... building. It numbed so that she felt she couldn't move, but she wouldn't have to. The Veranto seemed such a weak light within, whereas the ice… *one pace and they'd be dead; two and they'd never have been born; three-*

A shiver shook her and she found herself suddenly staring down on her own shivering hands. It brought something back, landing her in strange limbo between choices. *Kill them? But mercy what were these urges?! There was no way she could kill-*

Raking up her gaze to contemplate the men as though she was only just seeing them, she felt her semi-scattered parts solder back into a semblance of 'whole'. For a wonder the soldiers looked as surprised as she to find someone suddenly appearing in their path; a few of them even suffered startled expressions - and for a beat their formation seemed to break as some indecisive hands flew to loosen swords, whilst others hesitated.

*'A girl… she is just one dirty girl'*, their faces seemed to read. *They were Zanzier men… only men… not monsters. And still!*

Tilting her chin to lunacy, before she knew what she intended, she was moving - the ice within warring with her link to the Veranto now, though it surely had to herald from the same place. *She could kill them all, she just had to draw on-*

A sigh of steel penetrated her intent; Solancei heard the sound before her mind registered who'd drawn, but she seemed unable to halt her advance. Moving without thought, she grabbed one lazy soldier by the throat. *Slow, they were so slow! She had this-*

A flash of cool silver prompted her to look elsewhere from the hand on the soldier's windpipe. It surprised. *Somehow she wore the point of an elegantly long blade at her throat.* She had no concept where from it had appeared so fast, but the presence of poised steel seemed to cut through the strange mental fog, suddenly rendering her clear-headed upon realising with no uncertain incredulity that she'd damned near walked into the blade without care or thought.

Stunned, she belatedly released the red-faced soldier with stiff-handed abandon riding shock.

The man fell back coughing obscenely, but she barely heard. Shivering inside as the ice lacing through her link to the Veranto seemed to splinter and melt, Solancei needn't raise her eyes, to know who held the wrong end of that blade. Her freedom was forfeit: she would've recognised that line of blood-red stones along the blade's cross-guard anywhere, anytime. *Simaro had found her.*

Her energy faded like twilight stolen by the onset of night. She could fight… but the Veranto was flickering and her body seemed too heavy to house her insides. That hand held the sword stone-steady, the tip hovering barely a hair's touch from her skin, and he'd cut her before she could breathe to move. *She should fight, yes – but…*

As if he'd read her mind, Simaro shifted the sword a sliver, forcing her head up as though to remind her of the impossible odds and Solancei daren't breathe as a hundred scenarios raced through her mind in one free beat of the heart. *She had no choice but to acknowledge her situation it seemed, but Gods…*

As their eyes met, she felt her entire body slow in preparation for his wrath. Eyes the colour of new ice and chipped flint told her to push this just an inch - in less than a blink he would have her on the floor, gasping beneath the fountain of her own life-blood!

The truth made her heart drop through her chest: her mental ability to role play, no longer enough to feed pretence and the calculations were simple, done in a flash. *Mercy, but there were times where the Gods just seemed oblivious, and there were the times where they seemed downright determined to mock her very existence.* Upon her applied show of aggression, the soldiers' gazes held not a splinter of compassion and she felt herself waver on her feet. *What had Simaro told them about this? About her? Would they know the truth or think her a criminal? Given that this was Zanzier, would they even form a distinction?* Perhaps, but not after that small stunt of hers, she'd wager.

She drew a careful breath that barely stirred her chest, the effort burning. The tip of his blade at her jugular seemed to channel menace: a sentiment as real as the poetic kick in the head Kira'Cha had just dealt her! *Will I amuse her by dying today,* Solancei wondered, *would she finally notice me then?*

She tried to draw another breath to ease the tightness that was building in her chest but it was all she could do not to cut herself. Her heart was a red-hot knot of pain… but not as hot as Simaro's anger.

*It is a fine blade,* she mused semi-distracted as she looked into his eyes without blinking, trying to give him no cause for further offence, but her lungs were hurting as though she'd sucked in too much cold air on a crisp Tarléonin morning. *Yes, the blade was fine indeed. No more than an inch and a half wide, but with a fair reach, suitable for a man of his height and polished to gleam along its sharp edges in a fashion that revealed it to be Dragon Silver folded around a core of common steel.*

"Will she still fight, Milord?" she heard someone ask, but the man never got an answer. Aloud she felt like saying: till my dying breath! *But it'd be a lie.*

Her gaze fluttered. Those official surcoats were surely the brightest thing she'd ever seen any true-blooded Zanzierian wear, but underneath the padding, she spied a flash of hauberk. The seax was old and her strength waning; the men might look uncomfortable within their gear in this enclosed space – but it was also that very same, which would protect them. *Gods, and just where would she run anyway? How far would she get?*

Brittle with irony, her lips twitched to soften the rue. *Those men would not care what Simaro did next; no matter what, she was fresh out of fight!*

Solancei lifted her hands a few slow inches from her sides, the gesture disarming, *she hoped,* as she shifted her eyes along the length of cold steel to meet Simaro's again. She was starting to shiver – though whether from fear, nerves or weariness, she could not have said. *Smoke and mirrors – that is all it is! Smoke and Mirrors! Get through this!*

Across the blade, Simaro gave her a sawing, narrow-eyed look – the only outward sign that he'd noticed her movement. In response, she lifted her hands a little higher.

"Stop!" he ordered, jolting her slightly. With a curt snap of his chin towards the hand that still squeezed the seax, he continued, "Not another breath until you drop that knife, grey-eyes!"

Solancei felt her stare drift blindly to the stolen weapon. It seemed a foreign weight in her hand.

"You will drop it now," he repeated when she hesitated, "else I will slice your throat to ear this instance and bleed you out on the floor before feeding you to my pet Demonai up there! Is that clear?"

*Demonai.*

At the single word, Solancei felt her insides contract in one painful spasm of fear. She did not pretend she did not know what he was saying. And, she believed him. There was no reason not to. His reference to the creatures she'd seen was more than enough to make her weak with fear-remembered and in comparison it suddenly did not seem as bad giving herself back into his 'care'.

Forcing stiff fingers to relinquish the cramped grip, she obeyed, the seax falling to the floor with a hollow clatter, only to be immediately retrieved by one quick-moving soldier.

With a testy look for her face as he stepped back into line with his comrade blades, he tugged it behind his broad sash with no ceremony. *He was the soldier on the left. The only one with a beard. Neatly trimmed.* Was it fitting if she supposed he might have been the first casualty of her desperation, had she been her usual self? Well perhaps. *Tit for tat...*

Solancei looked at Simaro, but he did not put up his weapon. *He does not trust me. But then again: neither do I trust him, so...*

"Back up!" Simaro forced her to move as directed, his wielding of the blade careful and deliberate, and her attention remained indiscriminately his now. *Of course, it was not dignified -*

*but she would play this game of smoke and mirrors if it stayed his hand. She-*

Her back met the mosaic wall. *Trapping.* Across the length of steel, Simaro's smouldering anger still hit her like a gush of emotion made physical, his eyes as cloudy as she remembered the heavens above Ivanor before a snow-fall. *Mayhap, she should have fought him after all. Mayhap...*

She rolled her eyes away. *Well, it was all academic, as Palea 'the-two-faced' was fond of saying, and damn!*

A queer tick of emotion stabbed through her and her lips quivered again. *Smoke and mirrors... that expression would forever curry a whole new meaning now, wouldn't it?* Palea had been waiting for her chance to step up her game and Solancei wondered: in her impromptu absence, would Iambre finally let the insipid girl play dress up?

It was a queer sort of thought indeed, her head seemed full of incidental mush, but she hated how much she suddenly cared about that particularly stupid answer.

"You..." Simaro's viscous snarl drew her attention to him. To the ear, it sounded like he'd stolen half a realm of dark loathing and unspent rage just to pack it into that one word and she couldn't quell an internal quiver as she regarded him in wary stillness. It was a skill to read a person, but it required little finesse to understand how her next breath tethered on the scales of his mercy. *Danger hadn't passed. It was only shifted. Were she to reveal her true affiliations now, would he laugh or curse?*

The deviant thought held no possibility, of course, but in theory? *Oh regretfully, My Lord will need to adjourn this thoroughly unpleasant rendezvous by demand and pleasure of her Royal Highness the Princess Heiress, as the lady needs me to dress her hair... well, right after I neuter you with that vulgar blade of yours, of course, begging your pardon, but all offence deliberately intended!*

The thought fell on the wrong side of satirical but Solancei kept her face carefully neutral as Simaro drew a deep ill-tempered breath that rustled the elegant cut of his pristine tailoring which now revealed the gratifying sense of a costume no longer as freshly pressed as it had been. *It was a petty observation.* Sadly, she imagined there'd be no neutering done in any of the foreseeable future; the sword wavered and she sucked in a hiss... braced herself...

Rather than executing his own wish, Simaro bit out a curt sound that seemed like self-directed anger. Almost afraid of opening her eyes, she wondered with a racing heart, just how long he'd be able to resist the urge that seemed to curl around his frame like a red aura of temptation. *Seemed she had but one avenue...*

Despite the Veranto link, hard regret welled up. *Iambre I am so sorry, I tried... I still will, but I cannot oblige my Oath quite so easily and whilst I still have the present, I would live to protect the future, which means...*

"I yield." She heard the promise spill forth in a rush and saw Simaro blink in surprise.

"My word as I stand before you that I will yield utterly and completely," she reiterated, "Yield and do as you wish, obey-"

"Obey?" Simaro interrupted in a low, seething tone of cutting affront, "Sweet Gods, I doubt me if you even know the meaning! No grey-eyes - for ease I would End you and be done right now! By everything right, I should! I-"

Simaro sucked in a breath, clearly swallowing an urge, and Solancei could feel herself growing lightheaded as her life continued to swing like a pendulum on fragile wire.

A small bead of liquid rolled down her neck and she frowned. *It was too hot against her skin - he must have nicked her.* She hadn't felt it happen though and fought the urge to wipe the blood away lest her gesture be misinterpreted.

Biting back words that would not count, her eyes flittered to the four soldiers in Zanzier blue-and-yellow fanned out in their functional padded breeches and dark leather boots to match the strips of belts just visible below sashes and the household surcoats blanketing the functional hauberks beneath. On guard at their leader's back, they blocked the stairwell corridor so effectively that the space seemed cramped. *Four? Was it really only four?*

Swords at ease but ready, they remained steadfast in the heat, eyeing her now with the same kind of alert dispassion they would a prisoner on the gallows – and yet again, she was reminded of the truth. The jackal game had ended: those men were professional soldiers and the steel point at her neck no haitu that she could simply swat away at her convenience. *What Simaro did not see were the Oaths that controlled her though. What he did not understand, was*

130

*that she'd act as prescribed by responsibilities and pledged allegiances - and that was both a problem and a blessing!*

"I understand,-" she heard herself say, her voice a harsh, breathless quack made worse for the need to uphold the atrocious New Wood accent whilst preventing the tip of a sword from cutting her further, "-I understand that you don't believe my sincerity but I do not really wish to die. I... I-" I *will do what I need to remain alive and get back to my friend! Corpses cannot apologise to their friends – not even if such friend be a Crown Princess,* "-and I shall answer your questions." *And I shall report to Klaas. And I shall promise to learn everything I can about this freak show!* "And I...

"I will give no more trouble."

Solancei held her breath and felt a quiver in the Veranto. For a blink longer the world seemed to pause. Then laughter burst from Simaro: a rich, mocking sound that made her want to plant a fist in his ear. *But the ruby sword shifted a hair...*

"Oh but I swear by every known deity, grey-eyes..." the inflection in his laughter turned from ridicule to something of rancour as he re-angled the blade, stepping closer. "You are bloody right that you will do what I say now! Do what I say - and more! This is understood, grey-eyes!"

"Yes..." Still concerned with the sharp end of the steel, Solancei offered him a poorly executed nod. *His eyes were cold, fractured ice crystals that cut as deeply as any sword in their own chilling fashion, but they were no longer brimming with promises of death. At least they were not that!*

"Now I would level with you grey-eyes,-" his tone became measured suddenly - like a trained courtier, not without anger yet, but controlled, "-and if it pleases you so to live, you will listen. And listen good! Firstly, I would assure you that the potential you may embody will not serve as a deterrent; nor will the fact that you are young, or skilled, or a woman. Give me an ounce more trouble and I'll show you to the gates of the Void. Understood?!"

"Yes." Solancei blinked. *This was dangerous. Being his prisoner again would be dangerous and it could bring Iambre in peril too. Instinct told her to bolt - but her mind was more prudent.*

She suppressed a shiver to stop his steel from cutting her again and averted her gaze meekly. It earned her scrutiny; she felt his pale eyes raking her in appraisal, yet she pandered to his character, kept still, and something seemed to satisfy him for the aura flowing off him gained a measure of civility then and she allowed herself a ghostly smile to celebrate the success.

*Another day they'd have a reckoning. Another day, though Luck would probably have nothing to do with that either.*

# Eye to Eye

*So… another day… another time…*

It was a silent promise but Solancei felt no excitement at the prospect, no secret jab of satisfaction in knowing that her surrender was but a show of smoke and mirrors too. *The man was wary. Escaping a second time would not be easy.*

"Good then," Simaro allowed in the same measured voice of restraint.

Oblivious to her thoughts, taking a moment to swipe the film of sweat from his forehead, he said, "You know you ought to take a few breaths to silently praise whatever Gods you hold dear that I am intrigued by you! And, while you're at it, praise them too that they have at least granted you a measure of wisdom: enough to entertain the idea of self-preservation - but for those skills you've exhibited, your journey Beyond would already have been long underway!"

Again, Solancei believed him; her heart was racing, though now shamefully with the elation of her given reprieve, pierced by the inconceivable fact that she'd folded. She pretended it mattered that if she had nothing else, at least she did know how to culture her sense of self-preservation these days, but of course, she wasn't about to go thank the Gods for that - this was none of their doings – and…

*And bloody rats… she was not about to split hairs over beliefs and faith, either. Not with Simaro, anyway. He wanted quiet and meek, so quiet and meek he would have - because she needed to make him believe that he'd won.*

Outward her expression remained as calm and unassuming as she could muster; inwards, she fumbled like a novice to raise the shields of Veranto higher. *It had to be enough.* She'd deliberately lowered her gaze - like a true-born Zanzierian would have done to make him believe his victory, and now...

*Well, now she just had to keep this sleight of hand going.*

Mercy but it was already hard; she could count in single figures the times she'd been forced to defer to another person's will with this level of abandon – and it had most assuredly never happened just to pander to anyone's pride or ego. *But I am Iambre's Shield,* she reminded herself, *and I am not too proud to grovel if it gets me back to her!*

"Very well." he bit out, though she heard him grimace as though he still found multiple discrepancies with his own decision. She stayed motionless and Simaro drew a breath, slowly releasing it - and then her - carefully withdrawing first one step, then another, before bringing the blade down. It was a relief and she expelled a sigh. *One day I'll break his nose,* she promised herself, *and maybe Klaas' too, for putting me in this situation. One day...*

"I shall enjoy that we are in accord then finally," he told her with a gracious smile that could've belonged to a different situation.

*Yes, I wager you will,* she thought back with venom but managed to keep her face blank, ensuring that she did not move a muscle even as she heard the rasping hiss of his blade returning home with a sharp click to punctuate the end of immediate danger.

A subtle velvety growl ruined the moment.

For a merciful handful of time, she'd forgotten about the 'abominations' but even removed by distance and stone, it was a sound still rife with an edge of sensation.

It made her sweat with fresh terror. It also made Simaro seem suddenly harmless, and though that too was an illusion, at least he hadn't yet managed to strip her down to a mindless husk like the Demonai had done. It didn't mean that he wasn't able or willing though, but one ride at a time… *one ride.*

Seeking calm, folding her hands in front of her in a way that imitated Klaas, she put her faith in the now, yet not relishing what must come next as she studied a cracked fingernail.

"It's amazing really," Simaro snorted, hooking her attention with an edge of wry exasperation, "You see, I have had my men run themselves ragged in pursuing you down this hole - and that in spite of accounting for the possibility that you'd not recognise the small curse of this place! You realise the inconvenience, I trust."

Solancei cared little that she'd scarred the flow of his precious time, but his words did raise interest. *Of course, the curiosity won.*

Against wishes of better judgement, she said, "Curse?"

He snorted softly. "Trick, curse, magic… I never knew what to make of it, but yes: there's a knack to these corridors, you know. To go up, one must go down; to do down, one must go up, and so here you are indeed: foiled like any other fool, but further below ground than I'd have expected, and appearing somewhat out of nowhere too. My dear lost wretch, I would complement your achievement, if it wasn't for the fact you've proven such a damnable nuisance!"

So he'd been angered further than she'd realised, but she was too worn to care - the insight not important. This 'curse thing', however, very much was. *Down to go up?* Solancei suppressed a frown, the conundrum inspiring little more than irritation. *He made no sense. That statement made no sense. Instinct was to ask for details, but her gut feeling warned her off against trying.*

Instead, she wove her fingers together, the act a small movement to suppress unease and to better cultivate an air of resignation. Several words were on the tip of her tongue but she did not push his mood and he did not appear to notice her small struggle.

"Anyway, here you are,-" he repeated, "-in the one place, I should've least expected! Hah but the irony, grey-eyes…"

Solancei stared hard at her feet. The toes of her boots were scuffed. Lingering evidence of mud dulled the mute colour and the leather bore several artistic lines of water damage besides. *It'd take a lot of grease to set it right…*

She twisted her fingers. *Would that she could somehow sneak her boots into the general pile of items that would be seen to by Iambre's multi-talented host of people. Would that she could.*

"…and I think you'd agree?" At the sharp lift to his words, Solancei startled, realising that he'd asked her a question, but unable to hide the fact that she'd apparently faded from attention. *Fleck, her head was full of mush…*

"Look at me," he demanded with the same edge of danger as before and Solancei looked up, smoothing shimmering confusion.

"I would see your face and those dark eyes of yours," he continued with a poignant glare, "Otherwise, how would I read what you are contemplating?"

*Contemplating?* Eyes widening a touch, she gave him a guileless look. *Where does one get a pair of Demonai and how does one chain them up like that?* "I am contemplating that I am tired, and that I stink, and that I sincerely regret this entire venture."

Simaro raised his brows, imitating candid surprise, but silently pushing her.

Solancei cut a woeful smile in half and kept her meek disposition true, her physical concerns portrayed by nothing more than a soft lean to favour her ribs, and if the pull of her worries drew deeper the colour of dark shadows under her eyes, it could be explained by general exhaustion, which would have to do. *And besides, she was painfully candid now. She did regret this shed load of grief! Who'd not?*

"I see." Clasping the hilt of his sword, he tapped a thumb on the large red jewel at the crest of the golden pommel as if weighing her words. Solancei met his gaze – *be meek!* – and clasped her fingers tight like cord. She saw him note the small gesture this time, saw his gaze drift for half a beat before returning to hers. *Interesting,* his eyes seemed to say as he tapped the red jewel just once more, then turned from her.

"So I wasn't even going to come here today, would you believe?" His voice was casually engaging now. "However, since your antics made me beyond late for the royal merriments of my own court, and since I did happen to have a little unfinished business to

137

complete before the end of this week, I thought myself in the right frame of mind after all. Now perhaps it is fortuitous that I can invite you to play witness? Perhaps it will serve us both, I wonder? To further our understanding of each other, that is."

Solancei regarded him warily, not really sure she'd dare respond, but Simaro did not appear concerned as he twisted to stare up the tunnel with a pensive frown. Then, abruptly and without further word, he stepped forward, snatching a hold of her upper arm in a way that did not bode well.

She suppressed objection for the sake of her next breath, not liking however, just how the guards did not appear in a hurry to sheath their swords as they fell in behind the two of them - much like a guard of honour, keeping back a statutory five paces as they began to climb the obscenely decorated stairwell.

"Gods but I should have cut that soft, tanned throat of yours back in that backyard," he lamented to himself with an almost unrealised gesture towards the sleek-looking dagger seated next to his sword like a younger sibling forged by the same artisan. "Hmm yes… just as I should let the men take you back to the cell right now to have words with the two that you - well for lack of apt description – *tricked."*

His self-contrition became troubled as he looked to her askance with features posed on the edge of realised conflict. "Problem is grey-eyes that one of them is in no condition to take an audience – penitent you might be or otherwise willing to make amends! - and as for the other…

"Well, to be fair, he will probably be inclined to throttle you till you're dead, dead, dead - which, of course, I cannot allow and still get what I want, so…"

Simaro shrugged but the casual gesture belied the unsteady look she spied in his eyes and she was uncomfortably gripped by a pinch of her former angst. There could be no doubt in her mind that he was about to lead her straight back into the cavern and though he'd set a measured pace, unease grew like a stain within.

"Oh come, come now, grey-eyes," Simaro gave her arm a squeeze, "Don't dawdle, pick up the pace. I know you can be fleet of foot!"

Solancei smirked. *She hadn't realised she was dragging her feet.* Belatedly, she tried to feign an apologetic mien. "My apologies then. I did not mean to offend."

"Oh I am sure you did not-" by his tone, it was clear that he thought just the opposite, "-but I have guests awaiting my pleasure: people and dignitaries that must not find offence with my role as host. I've a small matter to settle but do not intend to take all day here, so hop-hop grey-eyes, use those comely legs of yours. I am certain you will find the effort worth it. This, I will guarantee."

He looked at her with the direct matter-of-fact lack of care seen in most cattle mongers when leading stock to slaughter, and Solancei knew she paled, understanding his 'honesty'.

Nervous jitters filling her veins with something thicker than blood, she said, "If you are referring to what I think you are, believe me: I have already stared at your 'peculiars' up there and feel no overwhelming need to repeat the experience. It was… *educational*…

but... but not all that riveting. Now, I'm no expert, but surely if you've got guests waiting-"

Simaro chortled, "Grey-eyes, the peasant nobles can wait a small while, so let's instead engage in some conversation whilst we walk, you and I. You see... when you disappeared, I swore I'd hunt you down and end the farce, yet then I take one look at you again, and-

"Zulari'Chi's heavy balls grey-eyes... even presented with your present state, I look at you and change my mind on a breath! Indeed, work with me here and I might feel persuaded to making you an offer of sorts too."

"An offer?" *Suspicions tugged. A moment ago he'd wanted to kill her!* "Forgive me Lord, but what in the realm could you possibly have to offer me?"

"Oh other than your life?" Simaro tutted, incidentally amused as she startled. "Ah, Gods relax, grey-eyes. You see, the realm stands on the brink of change and here you are, turning up just before all the excitement is due to commence - as though in some game orchestrated by Kira'Cha Herself. With the Lady of Luck raising my spirit thus, can one not be forgiven for the whimsical pursuit of a niggling hunch?"

Solancei eyed him askance. His light tone gave her pause. *And raised imaginary hackles.*

"Everyone knows the realm stands to change soon, but I hardly think there is anything I could do to influence that." Solancei tried to distract herself, working hard not to pull against his grip, but equally aware that with every civil step, they continued to close the distance between themselves and the abominations.

"Hmm…well perhaps that is what you'd have me believe, but I rather have me a feeling that there is a great deal you could do for me." Simaro held up a hand, staunching rejections as she tried to speak, "Of course I also have a roosting feeling that you would like nothing better than to steal that dagger from my belt and plunge it into my chest, so before we both lose, I shall make efforts to sway your disposition."

*Her disposition? But surely that very notion was ridiculous!*

Perhaps he saw, for he shrugged with a cool grin to sustain her scepticism. "Fair's fair then, grey-eyes: perhaps more aptly I should say that I would make efforts now to persuade you that the dagger should remain where it is - because if it does not, your worst fears might not come close to covering what will happen before you reach the gates of the Void'."

Solancei surveyed his strong profile, tiny shivers trailing every vertebra in her spine. She was missing something here, but what?

The way he spoke made her dread that he knew something of her ties to Iambre after all and that he wanted to manipulate this relationship for personal gain but in her core, she still had doubts about this theory. *Earlier he hadn't known her? Why would this have changed?*

Of course, the speculations made her weary, so perhaps this was his intention? She could hear the creatures clearer now; their dark, heavy growls inspiring her to recall just how they'd petrified her as they'd stared at her in hunger from across the chasm! *What if the next pace found them inside her mind again?*

Aversion filled her on a shiver. It was a feeling derived from both Simaro and the Demonai.

"All fine, we got off on the wrong foot, I get that, but just take me back to the cell," she urged, pulling him to a stop with her random request and an earnest look that could be developed to inspire pleading. "I have told you that I will not cause you further trouble. If you would have me speak, then take me there: feed me and, mercy, give me a drink, and I will answer every question you pose without fail. Please, my throat is raw. Small things go a long way…"

Solancei directed her gaze back down the mosaic corridor, trying to pull his attention just enough to elicit the idea. It did not work. Instead, he simply offered her a slight shake of the head.

"Oh have no fear girl, I will most certainly put you in a cell,-" with a sardonic smile for the air in front of them, he clasped her arm a little tighter, wrenching her forward, "-just not yet. You see, the company we are about to enjoy will be far more stimulating than a musty old cell, and certainly to be preferred over the bunch of noble arses and toothless beggar lords that currently await my pleasure! Fear not, the cell will still be there after we are done, and the nobles will too – they've a princess to gawk at and will not dare move unless she does, so as for us…

"Well, you and I will speak further of my proposal soon enough."

"But-"

"Soon." With a meaningful smirk, Simaro drove her forward, ignoring her faltering co-operation and dragging feet, and though she did not feel any pain as he clasped the top of her arm, it didn't matter. Her anxiety was spiking to a point where she could not seem to think clearly. His cryptic words should be of utmost concern, but already, she imagined feeling the creatures' ferocious growls vibrate just a little deeper than before and the animalistic echo of their ripping fury made it all too easy to see their sickly-yellow eyes within her mind. *It was a thing that took precedent.*

Simaro dragged her forward, catching and steadying, as she stumbled; stomped a toe against two consecutive steps. Her straining found him irked - she could feel the tension transferring via his grip. *How much would he be willing to put up with?*

After what he'd said she wasn't sure how far he might go and he was too unpredictable to second-guess. All she knew for certain was that he appeared to have some kind of plan for her; some kind of theory. *Still, what to make of it?*

As it turned out, not much it at all. The sudden gleam of naked steel at her midriff made the question mote.

"Mercy M'lord, there is no need for that," she assured him hastily in response to his leveraging the long dagger against her, "One moment you wish to talk, the next this? Please, put it away, I will not resist."

"Well we'll see about that, won't we?" He smiled leisurely, looking straight ahead.

Confusion layering up alongside alarm, Solancei glanced over her shoulder. She was crucially aware of the Zanzier men coming up behind them, forming a loose wall with their bodies. If there was something to be done, she knew not what, and before she could decide, Simaro steered her the final few paces up the incline towards the Demonai cave, the scuff of the men's footsteps resounding like the beats of a whisk in her ear, underpinning the notion that she still lacked choice.

Determined to resist what was to come, she drew a subtle, deep breath, slowly exhaling, pushing the Link to deepen.

Growls and the soft song of chains billowed forth like some unhealthy tune never meant to be heard as Simaro brought the two of them into the centre of the platform, and she was alarmed by his bold pace and calm expression. Impossibly, he seemed as brazen as a seasoned whore's relentless pursuit of a wealthy client, yet as careless as a king of thieves with total trust in his own right to rule. *Menace surrounded them like a fine mist to lend the horrid stench a palpable thickness - yet evidently Simaro felt no aversion, no fear...? Was it just her then? Was it all in her mind?*

Solancei suppressed a shiver. *The creatures...* she swallowed... *'the Demonai'*-

The Demonai were stirring with interest, shifting with a limber ease that bore no signs of the strange mode of conduct she'd witnessed earlier, but she felt them just the same. *Like a caress in the air...*

Tensing up, she readied for something – *anything: for memories to assault... or for her captor to go back on his word to keep her breathing...* but nothing happened.

"Easy grey-eyes, my knife is to help you recall what's real," she heard him whisper in her ear like a comfort, but his voice seemed a thing of smoke and mirrors too and her attention was conquered by an image of rotting offal – *human and animal* – as it seemed to billow briefly in the air. She tried not to gag. Then it was gone.

"So there are several options, grey-eyes," he whispered near her ear again, breaking her focus. "You can give me the information I ask of you, or you can die – these two things are pretty set. The options, however... now these will range on a wider scale, depending on what you would have me do to persuade you of my sincerity in this matter."

"I see." She replied, a flash of unrealised understanding running through her. *Something new was definitely afoot and she instinctively pulled on her link to the State of Veranto to prevent her reaction from showing.*

Serenity descended - *pure, calming* - suddenly she had to push to compliment her blank stare with a frown of confusion.

"M'lord, you speak in riddles." She shook her head, half an eye on him, half an eye on the Demonai, trying for all her worth to formulate a viable contingency. The earlier questions had pretty much been an indicator that he'd be interested in finding out more about her, but why was he so persistent? Sure, the expressed fascination in learning about her tutor and her proficient use of Veranto, would not have changed but... *but why – after all the grief she'd thrown him - did he feel thus inspired?*

Flinging about for something more to say, she latched on to the first thought that came to her. "I guess... I guess that I still don't understand what it is that M'lord thinks I might help with? I..."

"But of course now, grey-eyes." Simaro sounded belatedly enlightened and seemed to miss the skittish moment where Solancei mentally swiped at a huge black-scaled creature melting from the shadows to disembowel her.

Like earlier, the illusion was only in her head of course: it winked out, shrivelling like a worm dosed in salt, but one of the creatures growled as if thwarted - *perhaps the dagger thing really did work then?* - But she'd much prefer it pointed away from her person. *Simaro... the men... the Demonai, in and out of her mind...*

She was on creaking ice here: one misstep; one moment of inattention and she might accidentally reveal something she hadn't meant to. *Was this why he'd brought her here? To distract her into making a mistake or accidentally reveal herself?*

Inspired by the heat and crooked nerves, a bead of sweat traced down her temple. *If so, his move was clever. She'd give him that.*

Licking softly-salted moisture from the curve of her top lip, she found his eyes, "Please... what I mean is that... that I cannot tell you what I know not to begin with. What...? What is this game you think we're playing?"

Simaro issued a gruff snort, "Oh that depends, grey-eyes. You see, you might be forgiven once for thinking yourself able to walk the path of ignorance with me, but I will not tolerate it a second time. This is all very simple really. First, I would have your family name; your real name mind, and not some half-cocked story about Anchan'Chi and your vows to the temples. In return for that, I shall allow your heart to remain within your chest for the next round. Fair, no?"

*Next round?* Solancei forced out a brittle laugh, muttering, "My name, my name… but why? What will it matter? I am an orphan, who got taken in when she needed it – the accent should tell you where – or so I've been reliably reminded several times."

"Cute, grey-eyes, very cute – but the long game it is then!" Shifting his grip suddenly to clasp the base of her skull, Simaro pressed the dagger hard to the flexing muscles of her belly. "A name, grey-eyes!"

*A… name…?*

The State of Veranto shivered. As though the simple the words served as instigator, the Link chose that moment to 'blink'. *She felt it coming like thunder from afar, it was upon her in a breath: unexpected, detrimental…*

Mind clouding as the raw jolting pain of broken ribs broke through the Link, stabbing like a white assassin out of thin air, a muffled protest escaped her but it never solidified. In a blink her tongue felt too thick to speak; she could not assimilate a coherent word, let alone a sentence of worth. In the space where her mind should have determined a course of action, the State of Veranto seemed to fluctuate wildly, for a moment buckling her knees, and she felt his clawed hold intensify, though from a distance that could have equalled a hundred leagues. It made her shiver as if fevered, a strange new buzzing tone in her ears creating a vacuum within her mind where she seemed to spiral down, down, down. Surrounding her, slivers of blue ice shot forth to rise in jagged spears in her mind, solidifying a new detachment that made her wilt without a care as it walled her in. It was an unexpected sensation that sent her reeling, the Veranto failing further…

But this was nothing she knew; vaguely she was aware that Simaro forced her forward with a violent shove that obliged her to obey as her ribs seemed to ratchet against the insides of her midriff - and for a heartbeat her world tilted as they both stumbled forward, half-wrestling each other.

Seemingly without mind or reason, for a moment, she fought both him and herself to claw back the Link with enough success to kill the pain. It came slowly – as though called from far away and reluctant to respond, but then she had it. *Mercy!*

The Veranto arose like a choppy wave, uneasy and wild, before her control reigned it in, covering the ice, covering the pain of injuries, semi-reassembling her mind. *What the fleck was she doing? What was Simaro?!*

Somehow ending up face-to-face with him, Solancei performed a staggered twist to look behind her in concern. *The edge of the abyss was close; less than a few good paces. She eyed the tendrils of steam and heat and golden-red light that rose like phantoms made of lace and air - and felt a hollow tug of warning. He'd wanted something of her, but… but…?*

Confusion twisted her insides. She could not recall: it was like when she woke up earlier. *Mercy! She could not recall!*

Worming through the Link, an edge of panic tugged. Trying hard to right herself and sidestep Simaro to disengage, she experienced the jittery tap of apprehension as he countered, wrenching a hold of her shoulder to propel her further forward with a lurch. *The heat was blinding.*

A sucked-in breath became a gasp, apprehension heightening to alarm now. Behind sick notions of Dragon Fire, which sped on sudden wings past the Link, Solancei pushed to alter Simaro's assumed trajectory which already saw them both too near the chasm for comfort. Almost she feared he'd not stop, though-

"Mercy, what are you doing?" she flung forth on a gasp of exertion as he forced her forward another inch, their odd discomfiting dance little more than a scuffle and pull, with one of them trying to work against the other.

Simaro expelled a hard breath but didn't bother with speech. *Surely he wouldn't just walk on, surely…!?*

The mounting threat sent a forked spear of higher panic down her core and she bit back on a whimper of desperation; the Demonai were growling: low, angry vibrations just on the edge of hearing and it seemed to rasp against her bones not dissimilarly to the way her own broken ribs moved as they shouldn't within her skin. Somehow the dagger in his hand became secondary as she struggled like some immature goose in his grasp, somehow bereft of sense to recall the necessary Kizano move that might win her freedom. *The man was mad!* At her back the rising heat lifted the loose hairs on her head, like spirits playing the strands through invisible fingers; panic had never won the day, but-

She chanced a rapid glance over the shoulder.

The sight chilled. *The heat billowed from the rift like a shimmering curtain.* She heard Simaro chortle under his breath: subtle, rich enjoyment…

Survival instinct gnawing into her guts like a trapped pack of rats, Solancei twisted away from him then, fighting like a mad cat to evade the dagger as she grabbled for his wrist and pushed his arm wide.

*It was not a move she could hope to maintain the upper hand in. He was too strong, but she just needed-*

With a mien of wretched nuisance, Simaro clasped her wrist with his free hand. It might have hurt; she didn't feel it. Absurdly, she kicked him in the chin and his foul oath fled past her ear as he repelled her physically with a simple unrefined shove – a provoked reaction to counter her childish act.

It thrust her from his person with enough command to send her tumbling and the physical impact of her sudden freedom was freakishly final. The inertia spun her sideways and onward too rapidly for her to regain the necessary mastery of her own limbs in time. Instead, she flailed, stumbling over her own feet, and there… opening up like the jaws of-

*Icy fear shot through her - a burst of rapid pinpricks travelling like ants within her skin; incredulous denial weighing heavy and hot immediately. Death was calling like a siren. With crystalline clarity she saw herself going over the edge – she could not stop it - she was going to burn like a traitor, and like a thing of life and breath, the Veranto shifted inside her as though she were a blundering novice: jolting her concentration, cloying her clarity, smothering her will…*

Arms cartwheeling, legs turning jelly, the heated uptake of air from the chasm blasted her face like the snorting exhale of an ancient dragon, nearly setting her blood alight. *In the blink in between life and death, there was a world of all and nothing. Ice raked her - a thousand talons slicing her open, but it was too late.*

*A river of gold awaited deep below. She was going to fall.*

# A Perspective of Death

Smiling at the man across from him, He-Who-Is seemed happy with what He saw in them both for He relaxed back against the sloping curve of the divan, taking a long swallow of golden liquor from the alabaster beaker in His hand.

Nefer'Kemnebit bit her tongue. He-Who-Is had made His will clear and she could not spurn what her Sire in His wisdom thought best for her - but she found herself chewing on the idea much like a horse newly introduced to a bit, still uncertain of what to make of it.

*How would this Sinuhé understand the importance of her gruesome vision, when he knew nothing of her reoccurring link to the would-be lives of these people she'd somehow strangely come to know?* Those twins were supposed to live, the Balance of all as well as the treacherous Mshai's life depended on this! *How could she even begin to relay her vision in enough detail for Suten Hamu Sinuhé to understand?*

Nefer'Kemnebit hoped she managed to keep the dejection from her face but suddenly her task seemed enormous. Her Sire 'indulged' her 'freak' visions on the occasions she'd confided in Him, but she knew He did not truly believe her – a living God He might be, but He was not omniscient, though many believed it so.

Still, with her own Sire this way inclined, why would this stranger be any different from the others? Why would he believe her, when even her own supportive Mama could sometimes not help but stare at Nefer in disbelief at the 'nonsense' she'd concocted'? The

Council had told her repeatedly to keep her mind and focus on the visions of true value – not on fabrication – but this time she could not! Would not!

These recent visions had been too real and she must make them all see this – however, with this old Nefer-Senef at her shoulder she didn't rate her chances, and her heart sank.

Misunderstanding her silence yet showing a great deal of insight, Sinuhé rose to his feet. He was a very tall man, even for someone of Elvern heritage: slender and almost ascetic-looking, but not frail. He furthermore had that aura about him that made his advanced years seem but a trick of the eye whilst he beheld her, smoothing back a substantial mane of white hair.

He lingered but a moment in some sort of silent contemplation, then stepped towards her, subtle concern evident in his expression, as he knelt down to look upon her face.

"Dearest Sheriti, if you so please, you may call me Sinuhé or simply Sinu." The older man smiled, a kind vibe issuing from his presence and calming her as he said, "And rest assured little one: you will still see your Graceful Mother if that is what you fear to miss out on now. Indeed, please know that I am only here to ease your task, not to cause you trouble, and the Esteemed Watchéran is wise in these matters, is he not? I confess I might also have a couple of tricks up my sleeve to make your life a little more... *fun?* "

Nefer knew she had to trust the man, but her mind had a hard time adjusting. The doubts she could not disguise made their way to her face and to her shame, Suten Hamu Sinuhé derived the truth with near surgical precision.

The man's smile only widened through to reveal those interesting teeth and Nefer fell calm. Without intruding with her poor manners, she suddenly noted that just like her own, darker complexion, Sinu's skin was also different: like the pleasant colour of an old walnut and in that way at least, they shared something she might build on. She looked down, felt a wobble in confidence, and hurriedly raised her eyes to Sinu's once more. She found that she liked him, but this would be hard. *How much would she have to rely on her own council now? And how often could she sneak away to see her Mama?*

Sighing as if a little tired already, Sinuhé shuffled slightly closer and let his kind eyes bore into hers and she relaxed a little more, feeling herself sway towards him, but not minding the feeling.

Holding her eye, ensuring he had her attention, flexing long unadorned fingers, the Suten Hamu made a small movement with his wrist, then another....*before pulling something black right from the thin air before her eyes.*

Nefer'Kemnebit gasped; astounded. In the flat of his hand, Sinu held out the small object for her perusal and he waited quietly, giving her time as she leaned even further forward for a better look.

What she saw was a small, obsidian carving of a prowling black panther no bigger than the length of her thumb - and try as she might to control it, she felt an instant jolt of appreciation. She loved magic and with so many stipulations and laws in place to ensure the correct application, it was a rare treat to experience it first hand. *Rare and unusual!*

In spite lingering misgivings about her immediate future, she had to smile to see this detailed image of her namesake resting in his palm and as delight now filled her, she looked up to see genuine mischief behind the kindness of her new tutor's deep-set eyes. In turn, her own smile widened and when he offered her the small figurine she accepted it happily, wondering now if this might just be the start of something very interesting after all.

Remaining by her chair, her mentor kept the smile on his face but his voice took on a serious note, as he said, "Now enough tricks, Sheriti. I sense that you carry something important on your young mind? The little something perhaps, which prompted you to come looking for your mother in the first place?"

Nefer's dark brows swung high and Sinu laughed with a hue of warmth that made her want to grin too. Smile still in place, he nodded, "Dear One, I occasionally know things that others do no, but your face is such an open page that I could see the truth as well as any unskilled Seer. Dear Heart, since we are now both appropriately introduced, there should be no secrets between us and so I propose we waste no more daylight. I therefore I wonder if you might perchance wish to consider sharing that vision of yours with me now? That way you might leave your Mama in peace to enjoy a full day of rest before seeing her at sundown dinner?"

Nefer'Kemnebit was aware of her father's painted eyes on them both: watching her and Sinuhé's first interaction closely; protectively. Her Sire was wise, yes - the living symbol of their lands - and He loved her. *This had happened for a reason. It could be no other way.*

Resolutely, she made her decision. He-Who-Is would never hurt her. If He had brought forth this Royal Master to help her, He had done so with the power of His own foresight and with such magic at work there was every chance that Sinuhé would be the best possible help she could wish for when it came to setting the future events back to right.

Exhaling as she mentally accepted her father's choice of tutor, she looked Sinuhé full in his face, studying the chiselled lines on his weather-worn, naturally darkened forehead and the deepening of crow's feet around his eyes. His face was at once both timeless and careworn, a thing rarely seen in any Elvern, and she liked it when he smiled. *It was good. It was all good.*

Touching his halo of white hair tentatively, Nefer'Kemnebit knew that she was bordering on rude, but nevertheless she wanted to test him and with a child's innocent concern, she cocked her head and remarked, "My dearest tutor, we must see to it that you also benefit from some additional protective runes, otherwise you may soon be overcome by what I have to show you."

Sinuhé nodded solemnly at her words but his smile remained in place, "Well that is a kind thought, certainly – but you see Dear Heart, I already have a few to get me through the day and I rather believe they'll do me just fine."

There was no trace of mockery in the comment and with that her new tutor freely rolled back both wide sleeves to expose the sinuous designs of silver and gold that sprang from his wrists into stunning sets of geometric swirls and lines to adorn the entire length of both forearms, before curling like spindles of an old staircase around his elbows to disappear beneath the cloth still covering the rest of his sinewy arms.

*Like the runes on her Sire's own body, these were not painted. Which meant that her new tutor had been touched by the Maker, also.*

Nefer'Kemnebit's eyebrow rose high at the display of power, a whoosh of air escaping past her lips. "Oh…"

Sinuhé's smile widened, "My dear, I believe the two of us might just get along, don't you?"

Nefer'Kemnebit grinned then. *Yes,* she thought, *we might just, at that!*

Finally thoroughly comforted, she settled back against her cushions…

The Vision took her without warning. She felt warm and happy. *Then she reeled, the entire world shifting within and without.*

A blink later she was 'gone': all her view of the present day replaced in a split heartbeat by the dawning echo of the young far-seer she would one day become. *Gone was Sinuhé's face as was that of her Sire's, and the cushioned furniture, and the expansive courtyard; fear or concern never entered her before her mind took her somewhere else's in a rush of sensation and magic.*

Falling forward with no heed or recollection of her body's place in existence, Nefer'Kemnebit failed to understand that only her new tutor's fast reaction prevented her from dropping out the chair as she collapsed like one affected by a fit of illness. Images and colours, smells and sentiments flooded her awareness faster than she could make head or tail of it all, but if her mind might still unravel with the sheer complexity of her vision, she could not grasp onto reality for long enough to fully understand the danger. A pressing urgency to share the burden of her visions floated forth as her need to off-load the dense press of information grew stronger. Memory of life-turned-death and love-turned-hate flowed through her yet again, but differently again now because rather than the simple bystander separated by time and life from the event witnessed, some obscure part of her had already sunk too deep into this alternative reality. This could be about the twins again. She had a moment to hope it not so, then-

The world fluttered and…

*She opens her eyes to a scintillating view. Recognition blooms – an echo of her own mind, then gone.*

*Danger is all around them. And her attention is upon that – not the landscape. She is shivering. The Demonai has that effect. And the violence. And-*

*She narrows her concentration and looks to the man half to her right, half sheltering her with his body, the fingers of his left hand still curled around her wrist as though to ensure himself of her presence. It might yet all work out. Sword in right hand, the Mshai is speaking to someone she for some reason has not yet seen the face of.*

*The sight jars. The Mshai's pleasant voice is harsh – marred by strange emotions and… and regret?*

*She gets no further in her appraisal because in a blink he moves: spins her forwards like a dancer who whirls his partner close after a twirl to set skirts flaring like roses in bloom. The action is* seamlessly fluid and without pause – she knows a blink of surprise, her heart still racing from the danger that surrounds them, but-

Her shoulder blades hit his chest with a jolt. For a blink she feels safer than ever to be this close to him, then the feeling shatters as a raised moment of electrifying alarm runs through her when the sword comes up, faster than a rearing viper preparing to strike...

"Tarvia, forgive me! I will make this right..." the Mshai's grim voice floats to her ear as he holds her as close as a lover; closer...

It is a nice voice; she's always thought so and her twin loves it - accent and all. She tries to centre on that, but right then it is barely audible - however, she hears the strain of some emotion; perceives the spear of acidulous anger beneath. It jolts a memory. Hers? Maybe not? Their circumstances are dire, there is something very wrong: she doesn't really understand even though her subconscious is somehow leagues ahead of her... and...

It happens too slowly. She catches an impossible glimpse of thick hair curling long across one shoulder; waves that fall to her waist – her hair? – and her eyes drop without understanding to the sharp blade he is wielding already too fast for her eyes to follow; engaged...

Something sparks within her. She doesn't understand why he is apologising but as the blade moves as though in slow time to make every tiny movement fragmented and agonisingly clear, alarm ignites. Baulking, she begins to fight but it is too late to fear...

Somewhere, someone screams as if in mortal agony – not her! – but someone she thinks she knows well, but there have been *many screams already. She pushes at the Mshai though she still does not comprehend her own alarm...*

*Then the steel touches her skin. Silky; cool; hard...*

*This time she clearly feels the sharp Dragon Silver glide across her jugular. A caress so fast; so smoothly; so easily; so deadly! And there is no pain, she thinks; only incredulity...*

*Fluent warmth soaks her in a rush; she knows surprise; it's like hot water from a split water skin but red...*

*The incredulity soars but her world is full of light. She gasps just once. There is no breath; she might still be clutching the Mshai's forearm as he holds her tightly against his chest but her mind is slipping away and her limbs appear to hold no meaning. No breath. She gasps, and gasps again, but it is not coming. Her legs grow heavy. She sees only red tinted by dark shades curling in from the periphery like an avalanche...*

*Words of unintelligible origins sound above her... then blackness rolls forth... she begins to fall... and fall...*

*She knows she'll be dead before she hits the ground but this thought belongs to someone else-*

*The head-rush of morning glory makes her gag... she fights for a breath... a searing pain crushes her chest, then-*

With a sharp gulp of air, Nefer'Kemnebit felt her eyes fly wide, the searing sun in the Sabén-Heshep sky beyond the awning somehow too bright. The pungent smell of the medicinal herb, morning glory, had cut her sharply from the vision and with her consciousness being brutally restored to her, she wondered for heartbeats if something had physically slammed the door on the overpowering visions, once and for all shutting them off, because she felt utterly drained. And utterly centred in the present.

Yelping with alarm, she gasped and gulped in air, the morning glory making it impossible for her even to imagine the patterns of benedictions upon her own shaved pate. There was only 'the now' and yet... *amidst the grounded feeling of escape...* she still felt certain that she'd just had her throat cut.

She gasped, hands flying to the cut in her neck, but they encountered only unbroken skin. She gulped down more air in sheer relief that she was able. *The Blue-haired Mshai... he'd-*

A small sob escaped her.

*This had been new! Never had she'd died in a vision before. Never!*

# To Forge an Understanding

The heat drew a breath and reached for her with invisible arms of scorching air. Solancei thought she issued a sound – something somewhere between an impotent whimper escaping on a half-breath and a choking souvenir of thick terror that hacked at her vocal cords. *Gravity would finish it all!*

A strong hand caught her by one wrist - for a moment of sheer panic, leaving her to flounder at strange mercy, utterly unbalanced on the balls of her feet, tilted half an arm's length over the edge. *It might as well have been leagues...*

Frozen wide-eyed with shock, she teetered there, the abyss grinning like a predator at her back, the sheer jolting impossibility of her unlikely rescue throwing her into an impossible state flush between catatonic and euphoric. Simaro's face appeared an unfamiliar landscape of edges and hacked curves - his purpose here hard to recall as he clasped her wrist, holding them both in balance like some impossible sculptor's play with a pair of giant, offset scales.

To Solancei it didn't matter. For one moment experiencing a hundred emotions and none in a rush, the thunder of her own pulse struck up like the beat of war drums in her ears. She couldn't bring herself to move for fear it might shift his centre of gravity - or indeed simply inspire him to unclasp his fingers.

She witnessed him blink slowly just once. *Not a reassurance, but a show of control.* Her breath rasped from her chest like a file over unhardened steel, yet a swell of unbridled relief swept aside every other feeling like a cursed charm then – quite as though there was no more room for anything else within her.

*Control. The fey bastard!* Like some prissy lady, she nearly swooned, the heady relief rushing through her core quite beyond reason, except to allow room for a concept of possibility that he was only toying for his own amusement.

"You know you really should enjoy the view whilst up this close, grey-eyes." From some distant realm she saw Simaro's lips move, heard him speak the words, and as if he'd compelled her, she obliged with a tiny, rapid jerk of the chin.

*Why? It was an idiotic reaction!* The heat was stripping and it made her blink hard, sweat and tears causing her vision to waver. She swallowed a sound, hoping it too small for him to have heard as she momentarily took in the sight she'd previously denied herself on grounds of sanity. *Whether amused or not by this, Simaro knew how to push her. Damn…*

Even at an awkward angle, the drop did not disappoint, though. *A sickening, mesmerising fall that looked deeper than a sixty-foot descend, terminating in a river of liquid, golden rock…*

It killed her elation, scrambling up her mind; in a blink new panic bucked within, causing her to feel as though she might jump from her own skin to escape the situation. *Was she slipping? Or was it imagined? Were his fingers loosening?*

She fought it, but the urge to make a frantic scramble to grabble for Simaro hand and foot was more vivid than her next breath. However, rather than provide the salvation she sought, it might in fact simply compromise the stability of his footing and doom them both - and with the thought, courage fled. *Mercy she just didn't dare try - and yet... if she compromised his footing it would solve much, and more, would it not?*

For a beat something crazed siphoned through her, waylaying caution, pulling at strange urges, but it remained beyond her ability to embrace enough to realise. *It would constitute the same as throwing herself in front of an assassin's dart to save Iambre. That the princess was not yet directly in the dart's trajectory did matter, did it? Potentially Simaro was the dart: take him out now, and-*

The State of Veranto was still a stopgap between her mind and her injuries, but not against this new danger that promoted a terrible end of service and as icy blades prepared to insert themselves to sever the mental benefit of her Link, she just knew she'd fail.

The fresh strain in her neck made a tendon quiver in stress. The terrible hypnotic beauty of the lava deep below left her in a state reminiscent of a vulnerable child who'd tried to run from her worst nightmares, only to realise that the monsters were real and that they'd let her pretend escape for their own amusement whilst all along they'd still tracked her, tightening the circle of false freedom. For a moment it raised the ghosts of her parents from their icy graves, pointing fingers of wicked blame and disappointment for her continued inability to meet the standards of expectations. As they morphed into the figure of a scalding Klaas, a betrayed Iambre and a King Kaimar promising her the flames of a traitor's death, she hated it, yet didn't care, as she surveyed the rift from the corner of her eye, unable to blink. *Iambre was not yet in danger. She had time...*

A bead of sweat stung her cut lip, jolting her.

"So? How does the game suit you, grey-eyes?"

Springing her eyes back to Simaro's, for a heartbeat she could only stare into the face she already hated. *Were he to release her arm the lava would cook the muscles from her bones and disintegrate her body in a blink. Could she betray the oaths she'd sworn, to avoid such a fate? To live, could she betray Iambre? Would she?*

Holding his gaze, she wordlessly shook her head. *People became oathbreakers for many reasons, and most of them* – Solancei shivered with the near-poetic justice of her would-be sentence – *burned!*

Slowly, too slowly, Simaro smiled, the small almost unseen quiver of the mouth combined with an almost incidental but certain crease around the eyes, just enough to reveal a man settled with grim satisfaction through near-vindication. Still, she was not yet an oathbreaker – and if it stung that he'd served her a reminder of his capricious nature, she also daren't look away. *To look away was to look down again, and-*

"So there are still choices," he imparted in a tight, testy voice, "but as you climb, the payments required will rise. You hesitated, so now I will have that name of your Master too. As you know, I am not a patient man but I shall count to five. *One...*"

"No... please... please don't-" Solancei would have shaken her head 'yes' to anything right then, but she simply could not get her tongue to form the right words before Simaro gave her a blunt shake that wrung forth another wordless yelp of terror.

"See, I cannot for the life of me fathom if you are impossibly brave or simply stupid," he mused, sour disdain warping the mockingly-pensive tone, and the pinched channels around his mouth scoring deeper as his lips pursed with a twist in a way to persuade most that he'd just swallowed a disagreeable mouthful of stale wine.

As she watched, the moue of the lips siphoned wider, as did the cutting lilt of reproof. "Of course it matters not, grey-eyes. In any event, I know that skills like yours are not easy to come by. Do you really want to waste all that training; all that money? *Two*."

"No... no please, that is not what I want." Her voice was shivering so badly that she barely recognised her own words. "Please, you already know that! Gods this... at the jackal fight... I just came looking for a bit of practise; for a few of winnings! I play no games!"

"Funny, the others said similar things, would you believe. *Three*."

*Others?* Solancei knew her face turned the colour of ashes then - she couldn't help it – and as if it was indeed all a game, Simaro's smile widened into something between a grimace and a grin, then he stepped back finally pulling her from danger to relative safety with one heave of tensile strength and a suitably denigrating expression for her strangely malleable weight.

It filled her with a breath of heady gratitude – a feeling she would not have embraced under any other circumstances – but for the blink, relief washed deep, owning her so completely that she

166

seemed to lose a little of her former-self to the sensation. Of course, it stood at screaming odds with the challenging attitude she'd pitted against him during their earlier clashes; she abhorred the docile streak, but perhaps not as much as the way it had so easily been inspired.

As she righted herself on shaking legs that wanted to give way - and might have done so too but for the Veranto and Simaro's hand still manacling her arm - she feared what another push might do to her, and it cracked wider a fraction this new icy void that seemed to have laced itself into her core. It fed the queer sensation of displacement but didn't steady her nerves. Oddly, like a second-hand realisation, it rendered the sense of her Veranto link strangely 'see through', but she couldn't seem to focus on this, nor on Simaro's imagined agenda right then.

*Others? There'd been others?* She was too distraught to ask. Thoughts swimming in a lake of pitch that seemed to catch and weigh them down; the ice created distance, so much distance - but something hooked itself to her: wouldn't let her go.

The caverns' dark fissures were dancing as her eyes watered and the quivers resumed control, softly intensifying. Simaro's hand on her wrist raised all kinds of goose bumps; of wrongness. In spite of the roasting heat, the ice inside spiked out like tiny needles to penetrate her veins and restrict the blood flow, and the Demonai growled as if they knew that her terror was momentarily not brought on by them nor their antics.

Mutely she stared at his face. *There was something she must tell him, it seemed; she tried to draw the remaining tatters of Veranto closer, but…*

Perusing her, feinting surprise, then insight, he said, "Grey-eyes I hope you're not questioning my account here, are you? Indeed I can assure you I have had three other girls down here in just as many years: all so different, yet all so boring in their similarities. In the end, I gave one to the Demonai. It was in the early days and I wanted to see what happened. It made for an unpleasant mess, of course."

Solancei verily heard him smile as he paused as though to honour the memory: it was in the change of his flat accent; a lift of warmth off his skin. *It chilled her further.*

In a reedy voice, she questioned, "And then?"

He sighed. "Oh and then I gave the second one to my men for pleasing me with her inventive ways. Now *that one* was so fond of begging for mercy that it almost seemed an art. After a while, I was told she really did make a convincing whore, although…

"Well, evidently she stole a knife and cut her own throat. Pity too. She had the face of a goddess. For a time."

He leant close and her eyes flicked from the fissure to his as he whispered, "I am still counting… Four."

The coldness in her seemed to eat up everything else then; seemed to tunnel in and then split, then tunnel a little further: the roots of a tree seeking deeper and deeper with every blink, the filigree mesh that bound wood and life, steadily growing stronger and harder. *Why did the State of Veranto behave that way? Klaas had never instructed it might become like that. Was it the extreme situation? The stress?*

Body quivering slightly with the left-over blanket of emotional upheaval, she made herself straighten before her jailer-turned-rescuer. A spasm went through her chin as she locked her gaze onto his, feeling ruffled by the new tilt in equilibrium and status, but preparing…

"You see, I trust, that this is not a game then, grey-eyes?" As though he sought to prompt her, Simaro's fingers twisted around her wrist and she shook as a quiver rattled down her arms. He could of course feel it transfer, but seemed to ignore her deficiencies. With a nod for the rift behind her, he told her, "Indeed, I trust you now see my sincerity here? I tire of the heat, and so with that in mind, we are back to centre again: I require your name grey-eyes and that of your Master."

Numbed, she slowly nodded her assent. Within the depths of her, the ribbon of ice flared to a point - for a moment seemingly pressing to be released like a physical thing - and a shift of emotion folded anger around her detachment so that she knew she would be able to move after all if she chose to. *But she couldn't use that. This was not the State of Veranto that led to clarity…*

Gripped by soft shivers, the solidity of his hand seemed to hold her fixed whilst all else began to dance. To prevent her eyes from sending her vertigo she found a spot and fixed her stare at an imperfect fissure in the wall.

"I will tell you what you wish," she gushed, finally remembering her voice, his bizarre, nonchalant revelations still shocking her almost as much as the stage of events she'd somehow managed to find herself centre on, depths and hollow of all!

"Oh, I know you will now, grey-eyes. I know you will. And so, in turn, I will tell you what you wish to hear too. You see the final lass turned out a sliver disappointing. After all, there I was: introducing the scurvy trench to the sight of my pets, when she suddenly lost control of her faculties and jumped; a little left from where you're standing but still… you can guess the result.

"Of all places she'd come from Carlundula, would you believe; had slowly smoked herself a head full of dreams, I fear. However, as it happened, her one redeeming feature was that she'd worked Intelligence for the Knights Commander of the South - an informer, no less – and so she did favour me with insights about the good Tahais Isoho before she jumped. Quite a few. Ah but the poor thing. Guess there is no accounting for loyalties: must have been upset something wretched about her betrayal of his trust. An admirable quality, one might argue…"

Rolling his eyes with a superficial theatrical flair, Simaro sighed and met her gaze. "Anyway, as for what happens to you… *my number four*… it sits entirely in your own hands. You are the first one who's intrigued me - would that you don't disappoint me now! - five is just simmering on the tip of my tongue. Just on the tip, grey-eyes. And then you will follow number four. I pray you choose wisely."

Solancei swallowed, turning her chin slightly in effort to offer him a decent façade but she didn't quite make it before a quiver gave her away. It filled her with a small measure of disgust; just enough to help her ford the terror and the mush.

"I told you I would tell you what you wish to know," she reiterated, "And so I will. But Gods you might not believe me."

*Lips stiff as the words ricocheted from her mouth as if she'd been predisposed to saying them, she nevertheless did not know from whence they'd come.* Her core of ice was rebelling – pitching itself against her control - but she smothered it with the Veranto and felt the connection strengthening.

"And pray tell: why not?" Simaro issued harshly on a deep breath, though whether for her obstinate perseverance or from a general lack of patience, she did not know. What she realised, however, was that she was gambling with entirely different stakes now: stakes she hoped meant that for all his posturing, he was not quite yet ready to sacrifice her to the abyss.

Serenity returning by a measure, for a moment she felt lucid enough to see that the things he wanted to know, they… *they seemed too important to him, somehow, but… but if she was wrong…?!* Well… the man was as mad as Allziu'Chi Himself! There'd been others before her – which meant there'd be others after, too!

"I fear you will not believe, because… because-" *as if compelled, for just a blink she caught herself picturing the Carlundulan spy as she went over the edge, the image closely followed by that of the first woman's fear and terror to be treated like a live meal tray, and she imagined slicing her own throat with an old razor, feeling the rusty, raspy iron cut into the skin. He'd done that to them!*

She swallowed hard, continuing, "-because it is not what you wish to hear nor what you so clearly appear to hope for. That's why!"

Simaro snorted. "Try me, grey-eyes."

Eyeing his grip on her wrist, icy reluctance almost bound her words - *for what she was about to do...*

Playing on the reality of her situation, she stuttered, "Please, I... I cannot form the words. I... this close to that drop, I cannot-

"I mean, please, could we not-"

Feeling suddenly unable to breathe, every muscle in her body strung tense as if in a fit of fever. Shaking as badly as the bird she'd once caught whilst climbing along the parapet of Servangar's East Tower, against all will, she shifted her eyes from Simaro to look at the edge behind them. The tendrils of heat rose up, reminding her absurdly of the steam floating peacefully off a cup of Iambre's bitter tea; it seemed to make the air dance, and for an impossible moment the pull of icy madness tore at her. *Would she ever dance again? In a moment her heart would jump from her chest and run away; the bird had been none the worse for wear - she'd let it go. Would Simaro ever let her go? There had been three other women down here. All of them were dead! She should have made the attempt... taken him down...*

"Oh, you sure test me, but very well!" Simaro laughed with an edge of incredulity as if to mock his own persuasion as he relented and pulled them both away from the ledge.

He didn't let go of her arm, yet it was still a victory of sorts on the ladder of relief - the change in their position altering so abruptly that the air seemed to cool and darken in the space of a blink. It left her light-headed - the fact that she was a Veranto Master, just stabbing her confidence to the gutters, increasingly showing her that she could still not trust her old skill beyond the next breath – but at least her knees did not give way. *At least...*

Licking her lips, she said, "I... I come through... I mean, I was raised in Etruia, although-"

For a moment her voice shook and faltered - in a way it was fortunate: it made the New Wood accent more pronounced. *If she failed in this, the Veranto would not shelter if he should chuck her into that pit! If she failed-*

She killed the ghost-sensation of flesh melting off bones, continuing, "-although... although they tell me I came from further east. My name-"

Solancei paused, feeling Simaro's interest like a caress against her skin, but this time she kept staring out past his frame to the place where the floor dropped away. *Her death would be swift, but also agonising, and then she would be no more, and Iambre would be alone. The idea seemed strangely fantastical!*

With a deep inhale she gathered every ounce of strength, then exhaled doubt.

"My name is Cheska del'Duvraska," she told him tonelessly. "It's the name I borrowed and shared with one brother and three sisters who were likewise cared for by the family who took us in."

She turned her gaze back to him, continuing, "I suppose if you want useful, I can serve you a beer or sweep out vermin: the Duvraskas ran an inn..."

173

She trailed off, her voice quivering too badly for her to carry on, but there! She'd made a start!

For a few blinks, as she faced him with guileless eyes, the fear that he should somehow call her lie to light pushed at her, but she dug down deep then, feeling only a sliver of the Veranto she used to know, but it was enough. *It had to be enough.*

Another moment, then...

Simaro grunted, the sound as weighing of her words as the sly speculation in his eye and the modified frown of pensive analysis. *What was the verdict?*

"Cheska... Cheska... now part of me could believe that, you know, whilst another..." He eyed her like a magistrate perusing an accused thief for the truth - then grunted to himself and shook his head. "Or maybe I am just distracted by the Demonai? You see, they are hungry - but please... tell me more, grey-eyes."

Solancei felt her eyes flutter from Simaro to the blood-skinned creatures. He could not know she was aware of it, of course, but they were hungry, indeed. *They repeatedly impressed it upon her like a damp morning on the early, bed-weary traveller.*

"Where would you like me to begin then?" No longer bothered that her voice sounded husky with dread, and no longer bothered that she couldn't stop it from trembling, she sidestepped desperation, but it came right back, drilling craters in her core.

"Where indeed?" Simaro snorted as though amused. That slight, secretive smile of his was returning, lifting the corners his mouth now as though he'd just preserved a majority in a vote of

Congress that would offer the nobles all the rights of power - like in the olden days.

Solancei eyed him, the ice within dragging nails across her heart and mind. There was something perverse about the deliberateness of his behaviour in the face of her unravelling self, but she didn't care. *She had to own this lie: this cover!* The dead could apologise for little to their best friends and they'd feel no remorse at being shouted at. Klaas would not be able to yell at a corpse! She was buying herself some time with this, but she still needed to turn his mind and persuade him that she'd be of small use to him – and perhaps that's what she feared the outcome of too?

*Because if she did succeed, would he simply not just End her then?*

Solancei had known all along that she'd have to weave him a persuasive tale to get out of this alive, and that did not bother her, but Gods… *if she was to entertain any notion of fooling him and still live to celebrate her ingenuity, this dance would be a whorl of near-truths and almost-plausible could-be, bound tighter in construct and intent than two newlyweds – and even then it might not work. Gods… it just might not!*

# Where Answers Lead Only to More Questions

"So! At least you are ready to trade words for the alleviation of your fears." Lord Simaro gave the formerly-troublesome woman the mildly appreciative look he'd also bestow upon a new lead-bitch that had just heeled for the first time. On a whim, he released her arm; just as well – his palms were sweaty from the heat.

In belated response, the grey-eyed woman blinked, a veil of relief sideling across her glazed expression but gone too soon that he did not trust the impression.

He ignored the niggling sensation as he did the Demonai-presence against his spirit, and stepped clear of her immediate position, allowing her to have a moment to catch her breath, because verily he needed one too - though she could not be permitted to know, of course.

There was an unruly feeling of excitement curling down along his backbone, and he must control the sensation, or Gods knew she might end up laughing at him instead of shivering in fear. *Control and distance. Just a few moments. Just...*

As he unceremoniously used the back of a sleeve to dry the sweat of strain from his forehead, there was part of him that wondered if this blade-whore had somehow done some trick with her Arts to make him take leave of all good sense, but looking at the state of her, now he didn't think her capable.

He smiled tightly. It was baffling really, but the act of almost sacrificing her to the abyss seemed to have worked a wonder, though the calculated risk turned disaster in a flash, had not exactly gone to plan.

He pirouetted slightly on the balls of his feet to face the pit in order to hide a quiver for the near-loss he'd almost caused himself: seeing within his mind's eye, her mask of terror as the momentum of his rash action sent her whirling towards death. Anyone else he would have let go. Anyone not of such 'fortitude' - yet nevertheless the event had unexpectedly served to penetrate the layers of her impervious distance better that he might have hoped, because she'd finally showed herself vulnerable in a way that he could now exploit at his chosen level and for the benefit of his pursuits.

*It was not foolproof of course – he was not a fool that her meek disposition would be of permanent benefit - but it was beneficial enough for now: later was later.*

He half-turned again to appraise her current bearing and the slightly-stunned, wide-eyed look she'd gained since his revelation about the other women. *In fact, she looked ill as she met his eyes at an angle that made her seem apparently fearful of his next command.*

He let her mind work to his advantage, a cold smile cutting the corners of his mouth but never rising to the eyes, as he turned away once more.

He wondered if what he saw was real - *if it could be real?* - then found it didn't matter. She was one piece of flecking workmanship – *that was real* - only he hadn't seen this quite so clearly back in that yard amidst the people and filth. But he did now: those other three twirls had not owned a speck on her, and not just for the obvious reason, - but a start was something; he'd chipped into her layers; had for now tamed the wild abandon in her core, just enough to pull its claws.

Simaro killed another sliver of strange excitement that didn't belong, but...

*Gods defend Zanzier - was he...? Was he really enjoying this?*

Bizarrely, he thought perhaps he was. Her leathers were filthy, she stank of something that could've lived in the gutters of Old Town, and there was a bruise across her temple blooming all the way down her slanting cheekbone in a way that might have made it a birthmark, but for its mottled thundercloud-grey colour that almost matched the unusual darkness of her pupils – and yet...

The 'possibility' of her presence here earned him the right to look just a hilt's width smug – *a good thing too!* - because he was flecking hot in this damned double-layered banquet finery that had never been intended for this kind of pursuit, truth be told!

With the thought, he looked down the scuffed fabrics, and knew the clothes ruined. He wore deep-blue breeches – tight in line with Etruian fashion, but uncomfortable for the usual Zanzierian preference. Along with the cream and blue shirt and tailored doublet, he knew his attire ridiculously out of place and was hence yet again inspired to bemoan how much time the delay of this detour might cost him with the world above. Indeed, add to that what had already been wasted on the hunt for the blade-whore – and how, for sure, Angemar would not comply without the usual fuss, and then he might just give himself a bloody sore head!

It soured his mood. But thoughts of Angemar always did. *Prompted, coerced or not, this impromptu meeting would raise the old man's hackles enough to sow trouble in the wrack's shattered mind, and it would undoubtedly serve to make Simaro even later for the royal banquet.*

Still, like the near-accident that had promoted the blade-whore's co-operation, so could Angemar's last moments possibly serve as inspiration to sway the grey-eyed twirl further to oblige demands. *Nothing planned, yet everything gained regardless!*

Refusing to contemplate the loon Angemar further until the needs must face-to-face, Simaro folded his arms casually and shifted just a touch to study the woman instead. She wore her wariness like a queen with torn gowns on her back and smudged lip balm: head high, refusing to wallow in the perception of disgrace, yet with an edge of chagrin that seemed to transcend title and vanity.

*Was she Cheska? An orphan? From New Wood?*

There was truth in that somehow. For now, it was the best she'd offered so far, so he'd believe her. For now. But only since he remained poignantly aware that no matter the slights suffered, he did still not want to cut her throat just yet. And so he could for obvious reasons hardly afford to push, or she'd call his bluff.

Somehow sensing his scrutiny, she flicked him a dark glance, shifting her body minutely as though impatient, and it occurred to him that this seeming show of procrastination was unsettling her. *He'd pushed her; now he didn't; what was next?*

For a blink, he saw a shadow of violence ride over her features: as dark as her eyes. She looked as though it might give her pleasure to rip the tiny smile from his face, but perhaps wise or wary of the repercussions, she momentarily lowered her eyes and the violence folded and morphed then - as though a trained beast - into a subtle mask of simple exhaustion.

It told him it was perhaps high time to strike again; indeed he sensed this the moment where he should pull her back into interrogation rather than allow her a longer reprieve, yet instead he gave himself over to further observation because there was something valuable in that too.

*For one, how was she still standing on her feet?* Simaro tasted another small influx of excitement to acknowledge the roof of her conduct. *Because she was injured; surely worn thin! Most people would've been begging for medical aid or poisons to alleviate the pain by now, but not she. Did she hold a Link? Was he indeed witnessing what he thought he was?*

The idea both took the notion of pleasure from the situation and served to heighten his resolve. In turn, she eyed him without expression for the change he projected but though she held herself tight, she also sidled left then, carving out a little more space between her and the edge of the chasm. *Clever.* She did not appear to care what he read into that; in a manner of speaking, he suspected she thought it obvious. After their small game, it could hardly be considered shameful to be found with a good dollop of fear for what might come next, and whether bolstered by a Link or not, it was satisfying to notice her dexterous fingers rub that wrist a little harder to cover a mild tremor that seemed to have developed under his continued examination.

She was young though. *What if her mind was breaking and she lost it like Tahais Isoho's spy? What if-*

Suddenly he wished the men would hurry up and bring Angemar. He pulled a face for the delay and she narrowed her eyes minutely as though in calculation, yet this time he noted a feather of restraint in the set of her shoulders, in the subtle pursing of her wide mouth. *Earlier she might have given him wit and venom in that stare, but now...*

He was aware that the Demonai presented an extra bonus, but finding her down here was another thing he must somehow address. *Had she already known about the cavern; about the Demonai? Had someone sent her?* He supposed it plausible – but to go to such extreme lengths to find it? *She must know she could not escape – unless of course this was all part of some devious plan he'd yet to cipher out?*

If so, it spoke of deep-seated intelligence and commitment, which in turn meant that someone must be leaking details to the wrong people, but who? It could not be the Tuxaman loon – that fool stood to lose too much, and he did not think his particular handpicked crew had the mettle, nor the desire, to sell out. *But unless she was another of Commander Isoho's ilk, how the fleck had she found this place? Was it some kind of skill? Or was it pure accident?* It irked him he could not tell if the Link could've aided her – still... if things went well, he would find out!

*He would find out everything!*

As though she read his state of mind, her wide mouth twitched. Next, a hissing growl made her seem to forget his presence,

181

however: her gaze travelling to the red-skinned creatures, and her golden-cream pallor glowing pasty beneath the grime. *Hunt; Hunt; Hunt, the Demonai seemed to push at them. Hunt! Hunt! Hunt!*

Simaro ignored them with skill and insight. The blade-whore, however, seemed unable. She could not be Isoho's creature, he decided. *Her reaction upon hearing about the three twirls he'd done away with, had to have been true. Had to, or else...*

He almost regretted the need, but it was time to pick up the thread and manipulate her a little more to suit his aim – Gods, and to calm his mind!

"I see you are struggling for words," Simaro spoke carefully, cultured and controlled, and though she'd just looked afflicted by momentary paralysis, she spun her attention to him in a flash, unhinged emotion travelling from her gaze before she could help it.

He smiled, feeling benign as he continued, "It's a common problem for the people I invite to join me down here. But truly, there is little mystery about this. They are what you see, grey-eyes, and what you see, is what they are. Tell me: have you never before stood face to face with a Demonai?"

The woman swallowed, tethering on the cusp of speech, then swallowed again. *It was enough of an answer.*

On a whim, he asked, "When you first saw them, grey-eyes - tell me: what did they show you?"

She dropped her hand from where it had died mid-massaging her neck and looked at him haltingly.

"Show me?" Her dark eyes widened in memory of something. It was almost endearing.

"Yes, show you. People react to the sight of my pets differently but the first time is always invigorating. You see, they have a unique way of sharing their experiences; a unique way of communicating. I imagine they gave you a hint of their essence: something along the track of how they hunt; of what drives them; of what they feel… that sort of trivia?"

Cheska – if he dared call her that - struggled a moment to gain control over her voice, it seemed - then her countenance turned flinty.

"What I saw was hardly trivia," she told him briskly, in her voice the steel to match the flint. "Gods, they are grotesque! They want only death and blood! That's what I saw! How…? How can you name them 'pets'?!"

A shiver trailing down her back, almost rattling her teeth, Cheska clamped her jaw tight and pushed back sweat-marred strands of hair from her face. To Simaro, however, she might as well just have told him every secret he'd ever longed to hear and then some. *Gods be good…*

Holding her eye, he smiled in a manner she seemed to find unnerving, perhaps because he allowed himself to relax with the relief of his newly-gained insight.

"What?" she asked, obviously affected by his cryptic behaviour, "What now?"

"Grey-eyes, verily your words please me dearly." He sighed, a sliver of triumph sideling through him like the caress of a noble whore: enticing and repulsive. Yet, because she'd given him a secret, he explained, "You see, what pleases me, is the small delightful notion that if you harbour feeling like that about my pets, I guess this also means that the State of Veranto is not quite as foolproof as they conspire to have one believe! And to me, this is a most-dear, most-interesting discovery."

Cheska stared at him, her face bland. He'd hoped for a better reaction than that, but perhaps she read him well too? Was she beginning to understand a little more about his need of her?

"This is the second time you speak to me about the State of Veranto as though I should be able to comprehend your reasoning and will. Why?" To her credit, the woman looked confused. He didn't even entertain the illusion though. Not this time.

"You know of what I speak grey-eyes," he admonished, "I recognise the signs of a practitioner: you shine like a diamond in moonlight, hiding the true depth of your allure, but not to those who know the truth behind the shadows."

Unexpectedly, the woman's confusion only seemed to deepen, her eyes growing cloudy. After a moment she said, "I... I know a few exercises. Most people call them tricks, but... but why do you concern yourself with that?"

As though she didn't care what answer he might give Cheska looked at her hands: seemingly bloodless, but the multiple scars and nicks he'd spotted earlier, muted in the darkness just the same, apart from the long grazes that cut across the knuckles of her right hand. *He'd watched her punch the regulator Mitail three times in the face for those: landing the blows like a bloody man, with gritty lack of mercy, almost causing his soldier to swallow the silver whistle as he went down, still attempting to sound the damn thing!* If she held a

Link, however, she wouldn't even feel the sting of cut skin, nor the dull thump of bruised flesh. It raised in him a wave of hunger, something that he must still for now or else lose what he'd so callously reaped.

"I care because I want to know the name of your Master," he told her with measured calm, "And that is all you need to concern yourself with, grey-eyes. That and of course your beating heart."

The woman gave him a long droll look. With a badly-hidden shiver, she tugged her hands from sight behind the leather braces on her forearms. "It doesn't matter what I say. The truth will not fall to your liking. I already suspected that. Now I know."

"Perhaps," he allowed, "but why not let me decide what I like, and in return, we might yet find some use of each other."

The woman pursed her lips, dark eyes weighing, yet she said nothing. It annoyed him. He liked hearing the uncertainty in her cool strong voice; liked the darkness that scratched the surface and brought it low when she felt pressured.

"So you asked me what I want, grey-eyes" Simaro closed the small distance between them fluidly and Cheska drew herself up as though cornered but he did not touch her. Stare boring into hers, he repeated, "So what do I want, Cheska grey-eyes? What do I want?"

Studying her face, he laughed at her consternation - because he'd seen the flicker of anger his rapid aggressive change of subject must have stoked to life in her core.

Bemused all over, he smiled. "I think you have a pretty good idea in that clever head of yours what my desires might be. I gather secrets and sway support, true – but the simple fact is that you will provide me with something else entirely. Your name and the name of your Master in the Arts… those are the crucial factors here, and now you have given me your name… and a plausible story too…

"So what else? What more? Shall we unravel mystery or reveal slight? I know there was an inn in New Wood: popular; with a multitude of bastard-born children milling around everywhere, offering bread and water and laundry services… that kind of thing. It burned down a little over a handful of years ago - if memory serves, it was an ugly affair: people dying, others never found…"

Leaving the knowledge hanging between them, he perused her eyes for a blink, then said, "Tell me Cheska grey-eyes: if you were by chance taken in to tend taps and wash pots, how does one learn skills like yours in just five years? You know a few tricks? Well I'd be inclined to speak a little more highly of myself, were I you."

Cheska didn't even blink but her features hardened. "Perhaps one learns quickly when there is only one choice to survive. I…. I made a deal. It was… it was a poor one as it were, but when you face winter without a roof over your head or food to fill your belly, believe me, it seemed like roses and daisies at the time. People would fight you for an armful of firewood and I did not know how to defend myself so I begged for help. It… it was a mistake but-" she shrugged, abruptly changing the subject, "-well, the other day…? It will come as no surprise to you that it wasn't my first jackal fight."

*If it was an act, it was good: the sarcasm rounded to back a hint of accusation! It was a level of operative he doubted Isoho able to afford…*

"So you wanted to live?" he pressed, leaving speculations for later, "And you found a way to survive. Admirable."

"Hardly." The woman lowered her eyes and grimaced. Somehow she appeared to shrink in stature - a change that was mirrored in her voice as it became reedy with regret, "M'lord, life is life. If you fail to amuse the Gods in this one, they will make it even worse for you in the next. Right now you are the one with the sword and the knife; I am the one surrounded by soldiers who'd happily do anything you ask of them. I see no reason not to do the necessary if it will get me out of this mess I seem to have somehow landed myself in. Oh and I don't care for games. You might think I do, but I don't. I also don't care for speculations, either. However, what I do care about, is my freedom. The number 'four' was never my lucky number but if words can be used to balance the scales, I am... *hopeful*... that you will make this time an exception."

"And there we have it then, grey-eyes. That is what you want, and I can help you if you help yourself." He smiled and shook a finger at her as if she'd been naughty, "So you had a benefactor. The person who trained you for this, I presume. The person who ensured that you did not turn out like any of the others; the person, I presume, who saw your talent and exploited it, am I right?"

The woman nodded. One curt cut of the chin, still not meeting his eyes. *He hoped she would name Knights Commander Tahais Isoho as that benefactor. He actually really hoped...*

"I see." Keeping the conversation on one track, but fighting the temptation to ask her outright, he sighed. "Still, you'll forgive me I'm sure, if I confess my scepticism. Overall, this scenario seems a little... *unlikely?* ...if you take my meaning, that is. You're a lone girl, without merit or significance, offering what exactly?"

"You are implying that I should appear worthless in the eyes of others just because I have been born female?" Cheska raised a questioning brow, her mien laced with derogatory candour suddenly - he expected, in the face of what she'd consider a brute Zanzierian view.

"But of course – surely even you can see the merit of my deduction here."

She almost sneered at him, then. Almost. But she must have recalled the unhealthy effect it seemed to have on her health whenever she'd pushed him, for she exhaled sharply and closed her eyes for several blinks instead.

"Ah get over your grief, Cheska grey-eyes," he remarked, not afraid of practicalities. "As a matter of fact, I see you, and some people are simply that gifted – even women. So why not you?

"No, the separate issue here remains that you dare move to drag my honour through puddles and pig shite as though it's second nature to you; as though you could not entertain the thought of a public flogging for the offence. It is a brazen attitude for a simple hungry orphan from New Wood. Too brazen, one might say."

Simaro sidled closer, a minute shuffling that killed little distance because they were already close, but he enjoyed the effect as she shifted with the grace of a stunned adder to remain a full arm's length removed - even if the rock pressed against her shoulder blades in result. *So she feared his actions still, yet now she had nowhere left to dance.*

"And so you weigh me like the judge a thief put before him to assess her level of guilt: did I steal the purse of money from that merchant's house, or did I in fact also pocket the entire contents of the strongbox, too?" She shifted, both uncomfortable and annoyed - he felt - to be caught between the black rock and his flat, pale stare.

"Yes, yes I do. Because you claim you were but the unfortunate get of some poor bastard,-" Simaro knew his voice was rich with curiosity as he lifted a finger and tapped it just once against the centre of her forehead, "-but yet you do not have the attitude of a barmaid, or a lavender, or a girl who's been forced to fight for survival. Your face is too smooth; your hair is too clean and if you no longer smell as exclusive as earlier, you have still got a certain bearing; need I go on?"

The woman licked her lips, a foggy distance resettling in her eyes, then passing. For a few excruciatingly long blinks she looked to be rueing the state of her boots, but then she sighed as though capitulating.

"I was exceptionally inspired to do well, alright? Because that was the deal: succeed or die! My face is smooth because I am young and because I am not a filthy beggar!" Her stare found his: challenging. "And Gods save me, but I have never been known for my graceful ability to back down from conflict, and to be fair: you cheated in that Jackal and that is simply unacceptable – begging your pardon, of course."

Another sigh, this one raising her shoulders, shifting what was left of her unruly plaits where they'd broken free of pins to fall like beaten snakes across her shoulders. Searching his eyes, perhaps

189

for understanding, she shrugged as though embarrassed but her eyes also grew steely again. "I guess… I guess that my family never saw anything wrong with cultivating a strong belief in a person's own abilities and rights, and as for dragging your honour through… *pig filth…*" Her lips quivered. "Well, the question of honour is subjective! I was not raised to think myself less than anyone else. 'Honour is as honour does', that's what we used to say. New Wood is full of free thinkers and modernists. Zanzier does not rule me. And nor do you. Not even if you have a sweet title to your name."

Simaro gave her a perusing look. She made a certain sense and he could believe the sincerity of her words even if he was not about to tell her. "So who was that benefactor then? Dear Gods, no matter what your belief: what then made you - *a 'supposed' good-for-nothing 'blade-whore' from New Wood* - foolish enough to come sauntering right into my own town with the ego to think herself untouchable, when she proceeds to insult me on the highest level in front of my own people?! If you have ever heard of Zanzier sensitivities, what made you so deluded? Do you have a death wish?"

Obscenely, the woman snorted in some kind of droll amusement. "Blood and gutters: death wish? No! But trust me, if I'd known I'd land myself in this much bother, this is one cursed challenge I would've skipped."

"And that much I do believe!" Simaro exclaimed, then calmed himself. "And yet here you are. But with your attributes, why did you come? Kizano… Veranto… oh and let's not forget the talented blade work: with skills like yours, why not stay with this benefactor of yours? Are you not aware that the earnings of a guardsman on the trade-routes far supersedes anything one could ever win in a few ramshackle jackal fights?"

Cheska started shaking her head, but he paused her with a look. "Your benefactor must just love how you waste your talents then. Gods grey-eyes, does he not care for money? Does he not care that you pay him his investment back? I tell you, had it been me in his place, I would've hired you out to some filthy rich fat merchant to guard the cunt of his illustrious high-born wife from thieves and other 'delinquents' whilst away on business!"

The woman paled as though affronted, her eye burning, and his grin became a leer. "Well that is…? Unless the truth of it be that you prefer women to men, huh? In which case, I guess you'd harbour a certain fear that you'd get caught with your mouth on the sweet-meats you should've been guarding!"

She opened said mouth, then shut it with an audible click. If he hadn't known better, almost she carried a look of someone about to call him an idiot.

He wondered what he might do if she did. Nothing pleasant, he imagined.

# The Lie is Only Half the Truth

Solancei bit her tongue, morbidly happy she'd had plenty of practise with Iambre recently. Simaro had a strange way of pushing her past comfort and she must mind her actions. Of course, she didn't care what he thought about her 'preferences' – *true or made up* – but the fact remained that if talking was truly an excellent distraction from her fear, it also seemed to make her foolhardy, possibly because the strange workings of the State of Veranto that kept on stabbing her in unparalleled feats of surprise and concern. But perhaps she should tell the oaf that her preferences ran somewhere between dead and listless indifference, and see what deductions he might draw from that – *Gods knew, he was busy assimilating every snippet of conversation into some kind of profile of her life, so why not throw in some seeds of truth!?*

It didn't make him capable of seeing everything though, and she imagined the last thing he'd deduct would be the very real, very incontestable truth, that all and every preference she could ever think of right now, was concerned purely with the need of having a human wall at her back rather than that of the abyss or the Demonai!

"Very well then. I find myself oddly waylaid, grey-eyes, but I am suddenly in an indulgent mood, so why not?" Simaro gave her a long look, a small smile tugging at his mouth. "So you chose to leave your benefactor? Perhaps then maybe you hide behind other reasons than those previously pondered? Perchance, something personal that brings you this far?

"I wonder, could it be that you ran afoul of this person who supposedly supported you? Could it be that you are on the run from someone or something?"

Solancei looked down, aware she'd done so a lot, yet he seemed reassured when she did and it bought her distance too, little did she like to admit it. She only hoped she'd cooked this right though. She couldn't draw this out much further without being seen to overstep the line between 'fearful reluctance' and 'outright rebellion'. *For the moment he was fond of spouting clever deduction, but then...*

She felt his pensive gaze on her. Ever weighing. And yes, he bloody did enjoy this little interlude. He had not forgotten his demand to know the name of her Master in the Arts, he'd only postponed it by choice – perhaps because he thought she'd invariably give him additional titbits of information in the process – but no... his goal would still be the same, on that she'd wager her right arm and South Point, both.

She scratched with a nail at the scabs on her knuckles gone hard and dry, pulling at her skin when she flexed her hand. After he had his answers, she still did not know how to span the rift between offering him something useful whilst also remaining untarnished by broken oaths. *What was so important about her use of the Veranto? It was more than a mere nuisance to him that she'd been trained - and if he surely thought it a waste of resources, there was also a gleam of avarice in his eye when he looked at her. She didn't like it. Didn't like it one bit!*

"So are you a lady or just a foul criminal, grey-eyes?" Simaro questioned, tapping his bottom lip with a finger, his pensive frown now bridging the shadows in his eyes. "Tell me: if I were to check with the Law, will there be a bounty on your head from the Sheriff or will I find a reward lurking to fill my purse if I were to return you to a slighted betrothed or an estranged husband?"

Randomly casting her a sidelong glance, he added, "You are not that ugly and you are certainly old enough to wear a torque, but... well, I see no white circle where it might have sat against your neck; no sign that you've broken any marriage vows, so perhaps I am on the wrong track? Maybe...? Maybe it's back to this benefactor of yours? Does he seek you then?"

"I..." Solancei licked her lips nervously, met his eyes but looked away just as quickly. A Demonai brushed against her mind; *careful now.*

He was definitely building to something here. *Careful now, careful.*

Yet let him think her a 'runaway' if he must continue to look for intrigue – *that* she might be able to build on as an advantage to buy herself time - and meanwhile...

"Ah grey-eyes, you stare at me like a first-year recruit who's just had the sword knocked from their hand and doesn't seem to understand how little they still know." He offered her one of his coolly calculating expressions and this time Solancei barely felt offended because it seemed her ruse was working.

Ignoring the barb, she drew a fortifying breath and opted for an off-hand shrug though she managed only half a shoulder.

"Like your monsters over there, I am what I am,-" she told him, wiping the notion of pretend-shame from her face just a blink too late for him not to notice. "-it is very simple and I would tell you the story since you will not leave me be, but… but I should still not think you ready to believe me! Unfortunate circumstances led me to your town, and to your jackal fight, that's all."

At that Simaro frowned and Solancei forced her lips into a lopsided smile and crossed her arms tighter, mimicking him. *Time to deflect – and to inflate the lie with truth and life…*

"In verity, I am too young to gain the trust of someone wealthy enough to be offering the kind of 'cushy employment' that involves guarding the intricate parts of noble ladies." Solancei widened her grin, tilting her chin to the idea of regrets she'd never felt. "Rich men's wives can be… *difficult…* - or so I hear – and as for going on the roads…? Well let's just say that the dangers are many. I have no fast courser of my own to ride for the diamond miners or any of the trade companies, and they are disinclined to loans: something to do with them preferring that you ride your own mount in the ground so that they do not incur the expense, I believe!

"Anyway, they make you sign all sorts of convoluted contracts, you know - when you take out employment, that is. And yes, the gains sure are generous - but so is the compensation you owe them if the rocks do not arrive! I much prefer never to get that beholden to anyone, and besides, I don't particularly like sand nor open roads. Both make me itchy, so I travel when I must, but prefer the civilised living that is to be found in towns over that of the ripening stench of unwashed mercenaries, and relentless mosquitoes

- oh and criminals bent in Arbar'Chi's name upon stealing the fortunes they'd otherwise never lay their filthy hands on in ten lifetimes. They'll spill your blood, their blood, anyone's, to possess that envelope of uncut stones, and... well..."

Solancei trailed off, giving him a deliberate look of 'did-I-leave-anything-out?'.

Simaro nodded as if to himself, throwing her a sudden avuncular smile that made him seem charmingly harmless.

"And so you are here," he exhaled with half an incredulous laugh, "Grey-eyes, grey-eyes... who are you running from? The enigma intrigues me, so for now I shall still pretend that you are Cheska. It's a courtesy, you understand. Just a courtesy. So tell me: who is this benefactor? And what did you steal from him?"

Solancei looked down and swallowed. Somehow it was riding just a little too smoothly in her favour right now and she feared what he would do next, but she hoped she'd done enough to ride this wave of conviction.

"I... I... well, here's the thing: I cannot tell you." Suddenly her voice was shaking and she didn't have to pretend that she was finding it hard to breathe. *Get this right, Cheska. Get it bloody right!*

"You cannot, grey-eyes, or you will not?"

"Ah Gods, I told you that you would not believe me!" she moaned, a sliver of ice rolling along her spine somehow penetrating the State of Veranto. "I-"

"And yet here comes the point where I demand that you try," he injected, his pleasant tone turning testy. Shifting towards her, he caught a hold of her arm above one elbow, and she had to struggle with herself not to wrench it free when his fingers curled around the limb almost gingerly. As though he was coaxing a shy dancer, he drew her forth into the middle of the ledge, her mind protesting in fury unleashed, whilst her body took first one step, then the next, and next.

She didn't know if this would work. *Gods… if he took her anywhere closer to the edge! Now! She had to do this now!*

"I made a pact with the temple of Anchan'Chi in Etruia!" she blurted out, raising her eyes in a flash to gauge his reaction. "They… they trained me; they put me through the trails – everything – and I stood ready to serve until the day I realised that they were going to brand me. I… I panicked and I ran before they could drug me with the others and lock me up. They… they always find me though, and when they come for me, I run. Please… please don't take me back to them. Please…"

For one impossible moment, he simply looked at her.

"You might have told me that version back in the cell and spared yourself much," he berated her a length, "How old are you?"

"Four-and-twenty," she stated.

"Four-and-twenty," he repeated staring into her eyes a moment longer. "So you are certainly young enough, but your gaze is not; you have seen things, done things, oh how I wonder if I could be right. After all this time, could it truly be…?"

Simaro held onto her for a beat longer, then let his hand fall away from her arm. "Ah well we'll know soon enough, I guess. Soon enough."

Following his hands with her eyes as he clasped the tooled leather belt that cinched his waist, she felt the power of his scrutiny as he gave her another of those calculating looks, but she did not deign to challenge him. She was riding the lie. *For now.* But he was still not convinced. *Not truly.*

She stared at his belt. *It was wide as her hand, slung fashionably low on his hips.* She allowed it was a good look if the wearer was trim - and Simaro was. The blue leather looked subtle as doeskin, but thicker. The large gold buckle was inlaid with the image of the blue eagle of Zanzier in flight, detailed in faience and with crushed gems to make the talons stand proud as it plummeted to strike. To mock her circumstance, it bore the hallmark cost equivalent to that of a good horse, if not more, and yet it was as vulgar as the sword that dangled - again fashionably correct - from a plain frog, similarly tooled and coloured so to match the belt. *It was not hard to imagine him, smiling and affable and eloquent; the ladies would throw him looks from under their lashes and possibly hope to catch his eye and he'd know exactly why...*

Solancei felt a burst of revulsion and tried not to let it show. *Then rather make eyes at a snake and culture the attention of a wolf!*

It raised a memory and an unbidden image flashed through her mind - this one of her own doing. *Lazrin Sandborn had worn his blade strapped to his back, not his waist. 'For a faster draw,' he'd once told her with a dimpled, semi-cocky smile and a flash-demonstration.*

She did not know where the thought had come from, but suddenly the memory oozed into her, bringing sadness for the vivacity of things thought long forgotten.

*And I was impressed, was I not?! And not just because of my feelings for him; he had been fast,* she recalled - *only just not as fast as the two arrows that took him in the chest during that borderland skirmish, leagues and leagues from Servangar and Etruia and me! She missed that smile...*

Solancei looked up at Simaro, the image of Lazrin splintering. Now was not the time to think about the past and all the things she would have done differently. The State of Veranto was doing strange things within her indeed and she was trying to return her thoughts to 'vulgar' – anything to stop the wrong mental pictures from assailing her with further hooey - but it seemed... *challenging.*

Simaro smiled and she knew he did not yet know what to do with her. *Time... it was all time.*

"So you are young and distrustful, I do not hold this against you." He shifted his stance, pensively scratching his chin. "Of course, I don't for a blink feel you have told me everything yet - but I think I shall learn it all in my own good time, yes... and I shall inspire you to speak, soon enough I think-" Solancei's frown deepened. "-but first I should love to hear why you decided against using the bridge when you had the chance?"

*Bridge? What bridge?*

Solancei shifted imperceptibly to hide her surprise but her breath hitched. *He wasn't bloody done with her, but where was the relief? And Bridge? There was a flecking bridge?*

Her eyes flew to the edge, then back to Simaro, who raised his eyebrows in question, giving her a bemused look, and she blinked in confusion, when instead of answering, he began to laugh softly under his breath.

"Ahh, I see... You...*You did not see it!* Ah, but that's rich - of course, you did not! I wonder, if you had though, would you have chanced it? You are limber, you could have made it across safely – in truth, you still could - but would you chance it?"

Solancei could only stare. *He is mad,* it fluttered through her mind, *there is no bridge; I looked!*

"No?" he questioned in a curiously mocking tone, "Ah, but come, come now. I think you sell yourself short once again, grey-eyes. You could cross, I feel; indeed there is a ledge - well, more of a lip really, and you'll have to leap three feet to gain a footing, of course, but it runs along the edge all the way across."

In spite her best intentions, Solancei craned her neck to see past him, but he waved at her dismissively. "Ah, but you will not see it from there. You have to be on the edge to notice; guess other things stole your attention when you had the chance. Pity..."

"Yes, pity," she agreed with arched derision, the flow of anger and ice rolling like a poison in her veins to embolden her. *Pity, because I might have run the gauntlet and then the Demonai would have got me. Perhaps I did well never seeing it? It might well have saved me from myself and from an agonising death? Hunt and kill... they are so hungry!*

"The Demonai would stop you?" he enquired, the question clearly an educated guess but true nonetheless. "Well, perhaps you might live a while longer after all, grey-eyes. We shall see…"

He moved and her eyes flew to the dagger in his belt but he'd follow the line of her thoughts of course!

She raised her eyes in a blink. He smirked. *Oh yes, the bastard knew she'd love to try…*

Simaro shrugged. "By the way, you were right, of course: the 'creatures' as you call them are not my pets. Not truly, for how could they be? But sometimes I overestimate their fondness for my hospitality. I provide them with the comforts required for their kind to survive but they do so begrudge the lack of freedom, regardless – you see, they prefer to do their own hunting, but maybe they showed you? Anyway, the chains are custom-made as it were, and they will remain mine to control until I no longer need them, which incidentally shouldn't be that much longer - but tell me: did that sly bastard Isoho hope to learn much more, because I might oblige him!"

"Isoho?" Solancei didn't get it and he must have believed that for he waved a hand dismissively. A question burning her tongue, one she could not bite down on, she mumbled "You will soon not need the Demonai, you say? But… then what?"

"Well I imagine that they shall have their reward, then – providing, of course, they live for long enough to make it past the Mazes."

Simaro kept smiling and as though they'd heard him, the creatures growled then, low and fierce.

"But just look at them! Are they not magnificent?" His smile widened. "You should know they are prime examples of their species! Not easy to come by, as you might well imagine, but with friends in high - and *somewhat* unusual – places, I was offered their services. They are without remorse. Maybe they showed you this as well? Only spelled Dragon Silver and maze-designs will hold them for long enough to avoid ruin. The chains work well too, though. They have been attached to their seventh vertebrae, by the way. It cost me a fortune, true, but who's counting?"

*Who's counting?* Solancei gave him a sideways glance, chilled by his cavalier attitude, but managing to pack away the info he'd spilt. *Spelled Dragon Silver and maze-designs?* Had she really heard him right? *Spelled? It must hold a meaning other than what she imagined upon hearing the word...*

Still, on the upside, she knew Dragon Silver, of course – *who did not?* - but she'd never heard about such a thing as a maze-design, nor how one would acquire a 'spelled' anything - and for a heartbeat, his words utterly confounded her. Then she pushed the questions aside. She might not know of these things but maybe Klaas or one of her many 'associates' did?

"So you have bound them with Dragon Silver?" Solancei focused upon the one point she was able to understand, though incredulity coloured her question. "But those chains must be, what...? At least fifteen feet long? That's worth more than a king's ransom. Why keep such monsters? They are vile. Vile and dangerous. Why not just kill them?"

"What, where, how, why? Oh grey-eyes you almost sound like the Carlundulan informant with all your questions. She had questions too, you see – before she jumped - but perhaps the only question you should ask is: why not?

"Tell me: are they not an impressive couple of weapons? A while ago I asked an associate of mine for a sample of sorts to see for myself the exact effect of these beings and he sent me these two *Hyatt'Raah* as a gift. 'Hyatt'Raah' is their proper name by the way, not Demonai. I am told some call them 'Hyatts' for ease though, but people seem to respond better to 'Demonai', which I suppose it quite understandable.

"The name aside, it was a spectacular presentation: almost magic the way people became agreeable when asked to comply or else fend for themselves for a quarter within the cage they were kept. That alone was worth the trouble it cost capturing them, however as you can imagine, they did not thrive well in a cage, so I had them brought down here, where I confess they have been somewhat forgotten as of late."

Simaro's candour rendered Solancei speechless, and he offered her a savvy glance. "Grey-eyes, the answer to your questions is simple: I keep them because they are useful. Why else? What's the point of holding onto things that aren't?"

Recognising the analogy, she offered him an acerbic grimace and mumbled, "Yes, quite… What indeed?"

Tilting his head towards the two grotesque figures, he laughed at her terse tone. "Grey-eyes, I will allow that you are not only skilful with a blade but of a clever constitution too. I knew you wouldn't disappoint."

Solancei nodded meekly, but couldn't think what to say as his words of explanation gradually settled into her. She suppressed a shudder. Simaro's single-minded logic both chilled and confounded in a way she did not really want to contemplate. *The creatures' yellow-green eyes seemed to never waver…*

Simaro issued a chuckle next to her shoulder.

"Oh yes, they are hungry now that they have us in their sight. And they won't forget our scent, either. In fact, I've been told that they will remember the smell of prey that manages to escape them. In fact, I've been told the saying goes somewhere along the lines of, 'A hunting Hyatt might lose you from sight, but never from flight'. Even the best-bred hunting-cat could not manage such an impressive feat. Truly, what's not to admire?"

Solancei nodded again. She was not impressed though. She was petrified. *He was suddenly volunteering all this information a little too easily; why?* She made herself not care about the reasons but the possibilities boiled in the back of her mind, regardless. In a blink of clear wherewithal, however, she realised that for Klaas, she had an obligation to get what details she could - even when she much preferred not knowing another single fact about these creatures. *What had he just called them? Hyatt'Raah, was it? She'd never heard that term before. But know thy enemy…*

"The name 'Hyatt' is interesting but unfamiliar?" she croaked out. "Where… from where do they originate?"

Simaro smiled and she felt a satisfied smugness vibrate off him as though in waves. Tsking, he said, "Grey-eyes... and here I was thinking you were a clever one. This is going well but just like you, I will not reveal all my secrets at once. Fair's fair, no?"

"That depends," she retorted, if weakly. Did he think that by having 'amicable' talks, they would just exchange facts? Swap stories like a pair of soldiers in their cups? *What response could she possibly give? What? This was one of the strangest conversations she'd ever had. What would he do next?*

But Simaro never pushed her further. The sudden sounds of commotion from the tunnel introduced a natural, if odd, interlude that turned their attention.

"Ah, here we are!" Simaro's face lit up and Solancei found herself reluctantly copying him as he slowly turned to face the entrance of the mosaic tunnel. *Mercy... indeed, now what?*

Stomach already knotting with apprehension, she glanced at him.

"Oh this is our guest of honour arriving," he informed her in response to the look received, "Now let's see if we cannot forge an even deeper understanding you and I. Let's see..."

# Solancei's Memoirs

The Province of Tarléon.
Ocean's End.
Summer of 800 P. C. W

Alright, so you might think all sorts of unpleasant thoughts about me now – I know I would, were I you.

And so, in fairness, by now, you will probably at best feel utterly ashamed of me – in fact, you'll most likely hate my every decision thus far made.

The thing is: I don't blame you. I never will – not even when (in all likelihood), you would probably prefer to see me dead for the offences and hurt I have caused, but in spite all that; in spite my many 'shortfalls' and 'wrong turns', I still bet that you're not quite ready to believe that I am a coward too.

In fact, I bet (in spite it all) you still believed my backbone strong and my purpose set clear, but I am sorry to disappoint you yet again. I am sorry in more ways than one. *So sorry…*

In this instant; in this very moment; the carved red-horn pen is poised above the ivory parchment to write on as I intended, but I just cannot. The embossed royal heraldry on the procured sheet draw my attention: the gold-leaf enhanced lines seem to swim as I look down – and I wish I could say it's because I'm drunk on that heady wine I sent for, but unfortunately it is not yet so.

The wine – though exquisite – tastes like vinegar when I swallow and yet I have never drunk so freely before, because in this moment I am indeed a coward and I am indeed aiming to get drunk, if for no other purpose than to blur the edges of my unwanted memories enough to set me above them.

See, just thinking about the mad vision-like dream that kicked off in that sledge on the day of the funeral, somehow turns my bowels to slush, because it makes me realise that this began such a very long time ago. It also makes me suspicious that I was probably always going to end up here: a failure in some ways, a hero in others, but forever cursed to acknowledge that pretty much anyone or anything I'll ever long to care for, will most likely be snatched from me the moment I dare believe my new fortune might hold.

It is a thing to make even the strongest weary. But then, atop of this, there is also the lingering edge of horror that continued to steep me for years after that shadowy spear drove the images of that fatal accident into me. I am none too keen to rake up the details. I cannot help it – I just am not.

See, a hag-ridden figment of my imagination, I could have coped with, for children are cursed to be blighted by vivid imaginations and my dread would have naturally faded with time – however, what I saw in that 'dream' was not a figment of my overactive imagination that had been driven by whispers and terror to take the form of a vivid nightmare. *No, what I saw was the 'Truth'! I was somehow 'transported' to occupy a front seat to bear 'witness', and...*

And so I saw what my father's steward Rainan had only been offered glimpses of in the reports. Those reports had been bad enough that he'd still sought to shield me from the details, and the Maker bless him with good fortune for the attempted kindness!

I sit here now, and I wish that I could 'un-see' and 'un-feel' everything about that 'accident'. The Maker forgive me, but by the same token; by everything that's gone, I sit here with my rich red wine that I will drink to the dregs and order more, and I wish that I could just hide away now in my old chambers and never again set foot back in the world.

But I know that you somehow thought me stronger than this, and mercy, I am, and I will be. When you read this, you will already know I do not break my promises – and I promised I'd tell you about the accident that was no accident, and I will – just as I will not hide, but...

Well mercy, here I am - still drinking that rich Zanzierian red, regardless of all that continues to stir and transpire in the world. I cannot stay in Servangar now any more than I could before, but I will pretend it is otherwise for a quarter longer, because for now, I am relatively safe and a little too happy staying in the present. See here in my old chambers, I can pretend for just a little longer that the bittersweet feelings inside are a simple product of my exhausted state of mind and that I will be right as rain after a good night's sleep; I can pretend... *a lot.*

However, a few days from now I must chase the Horizon to seek out the Sabén-Heshep – and the Maker be good: Iambre! And by everything that's silvered and worth breathing for, I thank Alérathnar for that immense mercy, too! Yet, after this evening, there will be very little pretending of any kind for a while. When I go from here the fight will carry on, for it has not really stopped, and it can be no other way, but not tonight; not for the time it'll take me to empty this flacon of good wine in front of me. *For now, there's the illusion of peace, and the oblivion of wine, and the comfort of solitude. It's what I get these days – and fleck... I will take it. For that quarter of an hour longer, I will take it!*

The accident that was not an accident was just the beginning, yes - and I will not forget what I promised to relay - but for moments longer, just let me have my wine, and my good memories, whilst I pretend that I still know nothing of loss, or dragons, or magic, or war, or even... even you.

Solancei

Thank you for reading!

☺

The story will continue in Episode 4: Running the Gauntlet

**Available Now**


Enjoyed the book?
If so, could you leave a short review on Amazon or Goodreads?
Reviews are the magic that keeps authors writing and improving.


For glossaries, maps, and more, visit the author's official website on

www.llthomsen.com

# And finally...

## *Curious about the world of Ostravah?*

### *Want to keep in touch?*

For glossaries, maps, and more, please visit my official author website

Here you can also join my **exclusive newsletter** 'Thrills & Spills' to receive extra insider info, updates, freebies, exclusive offers and giveaways,

www.llthomsen.com

## Also feel free to contact me via...

I would always love to hear from you and all constructive feedback is welcome!

facebook.com/themissingshield/

facebook.com/linda.thomsen.12979

twitter.com/LLThomsen1

instagram.com/llthomsen/?hl=en

pinterest.co.uk/llthomsen7589/

goodreads.com/LLThomsen

\*\*\*

# The Missing Shield Series

This story begins in Episode 1 of The Missing Shield.

Below is the full list of books in the series in order of release.

- A Change of Rules – Episode 1
- Unexpected Bargain – Episode 2
- A Perspective of Death – Episode 3
- Running the Gauntlet – Episode 4
- Notions of Risk – Episode 5
- The Final Card - Episode 6
- The Lure of an Ancient Fable – Episode 7
- All in a Day's Work – Episode 8

# And coming up soon in 2020...

- The Way Star –Episode 9
- All Thieves' Honour – Episode 10
- The Neidar Ba'raie – Episode 11

This will complete The Missing Shield – Vol 1 of 'The Veil Keepers Quest'.

***

# New!

Also NOW available: **The Missing Shield, Part 1** - Author's Preferred Edition box set, which includes episodes 1 – 6.
Only available as eBook and on KU.

***

means, electronic, mechanical, recording or otherwise, without the prior written permission of the copyright holder.

*****